THE INNKEEPER

THE INNKEEPER

D. Woody Walker

Pentland Press, Inc.
www.pentlandpressusa.com

PUBLISHED BY PENTLAND PRESS, INC.
5122 Bur Oak Circle, Raleigh, North Carolina 27612
United States of America
919-782-0281

ISBN 1-57197-281-1

Library of Congress Control Number: 2001 131181

Printed in the United States of America

To Jody
and the hardworking and unappreciated people in the hospitality industry

In Loving Memory Of

Susan L. Matthews
and
Mary Ann Reade

A Special Thanks To

Jacqueline Hayes
and
Tammy Garland

In the beginning . . .

The Bethlehem Inn of Judea, some two thousand years ago, became the first roadside inn to "overbook." The innkeeper informed the weary travelers known as Mary and Joseph that there was "no room at the inn." Oh, if he only knew the VIP that occupied the stable suite. That innkeeper wasn't much as an entrepreneur. Just think of the opportunities and the honor that he missed—The Star Suite, "J.C. slept here," The First Christmas Gift Shop, as well as other marketing opportunities.

The Innkeeper is based upon fact with some of the names being changed to protect the innocent as well as the guilty!

CHAPTER 1
TAMPA, FLORIDA
1961

Ding, Ding, Ding—Front! "Yes, sir," I answered smartly.

Charles handed me the key and said, "Chance, would you please show Mr. Sabitino to Suite 214?"

"Yes, sir, with pleasure!" As the guest and I were walking to his room, Mr. Sabitino asked if I could get him a "broad" for the evening. Since I was from an old-fashioned Baptist family and only on the job for one week, I didn't know what he meant at first. I said, "Sir?"

Mr. Sabitino said, "A hooker, kid!"

Of course, I told him absolutely not!

He said, "Listen, tell Luís to call me ASAP!"

I said, "Yes, sir," and headed toward the bell stand. Luís, the bell captain, was a suave, smooth, handsome, forty-year-old Latin. Luís hired and trained me, as well as my best friend Jolly Jordan. He had not informed us about his other businesses.

Jolly and I were just about the only non-Latins employed, except the general manager, Mr. Sid Levine. I should have surmised that Luís did not buy his Cadillac on tips since we were only paid fifty cents per hour.

Luís happened to have taken that evening off, so I called him at home and left a message. He arrived at the hotel within thirty minutes, at which time I informed him about my conversation with Mr. Sabitino. Instead of being upset and losing his Latin temper, he smiled and said that he would educate me to the workings of the Tahitian Hotel and Resort. Luís said, "Let's take a walk." Since he was my immediate supervisor, we walked. We casually walked down the hall to the poolside area.

Luís began by informing me that the property was owned by the "Family." He continued to explain how things worked. "If a guest asks for a lady of the evening, merely send them to the Polynesian Lounge and have him ask for a 'satin doll.' This applies to our new guests only after we have verified their registration. If it is one of our regular guests, such as Mr. Sabitino, call this number, 555-3441, and give the guest's name and room number. This ends your responsibility. At the end of the week, you will receive an envelope. You got it, kid?"

"Yes, sir."

"Alright, get back to work," replied Luís as he smiled and winked at me.

I enjoyed the environment of the hotel with its tropical-themed decor and atmosphere. It was absolutely beautiful with its lush landscaping and gardens accented by lighted torches and waterfalls. The lobby was gorgeously decorated with flowers and live talking parrots. The hotel featured a show room, a swinging lounge and a tiki poolside bar, two great restaurants, and large meeting facilities.

Speaking of parrots, we had one bird named José. The management staff assumed that Jolly and I taught him to speak. Not true! As the guests approached and began to talk to José, he would say, "Do you wanna screw?" We missed José.

It was a very exciting place to work for this twenty-year-old college kid. This was the "in place" for the city called "Little Chicago." Here we saw and served celebrities, politicians, and dignitaries, as well as regular hotel guests. We met a few movie stars, entertainers, and sports stars. Tampa was where the Cincinnati Reds trained, while across the bay the New York Yankees trained in St. Petersburg. One warm spring evening while Jolly and I were on duty we saw the great Mickey Mantle, Whitey Ford, and Yogi Berra come in the lobby and head toward the lounge. Jolly was not the sports nut that I was, so I sneaked into the lounge to get their autographs. As I approached my heroes, they were surrounded by fans, including gorgeous women. They were having a boisterous good time, so I didn't bother them and thought I may catch them on their way out—with any luck. No such luck! After a few hours of drinking, my heroes went out the side door of the lobby with their new "blonde friends."

Since the Yanks were playing a home game the next day, I had to go see how the "Boys of Summer" performed. I talked a couple of my buddies into skipping class and going to the game with me. As expected the Mick had three hits including a homer, Yogi was outstanding as well. Whitey didn't pitch but was in the bullpen. I told my pals about the night before, and we all agreed—that's real ballplayers! Of course, we had our own local celebrities—

Tony Romeo, The Rockers, The Eden Roc, Sam and Dave, Tony LaRusso, Lou Pinella, Rick Cacaras, and the Traficanto family.

I always looked forward to the Italian gentlemen coming in to the hotel because they were big tippers. They loved to impress their "bimbos" by snapping their fingers, throwing me a couple of bucks, and saying, "Kid, park my car!" It took me a while to get back in the groove after seeing a gangster's car blow up on TV. I really did not want to retrieve their vehicles from the car park. But the tips were good, especially the envelopes at the end of each week. Now I knew how Luís could drive his Caddy. He had his fingers in everything. But he did teach me how to be a first-class bellhop as well as a hustler. We also drove airport shuttle, which was a great opportunity to feel out the guests to see if they were strictly business. They would always let you know what they wanted—food, booze, gambling, or sex.

On one breezy, humid summer evening I received an airport "run" that turned out to be a night to remember. As I approached the TWA baggage area in our brightly colored van, I spotted a breathtaking, well-stacked woman! She was flagging the "kid" down! I pulled in just ahead of a yellow taxi. She smiled. I bounced out of the van and asked if she was going to the Tahitian. Again she smiled and winked. I puffed out, smiled, winked, and grabbed her heavy bags as if they were feather pillows. I loaded her luggage in the rear of the van and excitedly headed to open the door for the lady. To my surprise, this gorgeous woman in her early thirties was sitting in the passenger's seat. As we were driving back to the hotel, I introduced myself and asked her name. She licked her sensuous red lips and said, "Honey, you can call me Cha-Cha." When I began to tell her about the Tampa area, she interrupted me by putting her soft, pretty hand on my thigh and with a slight Spanish accent asked, "Where's the action?" And of course, being a rock-n-roll college boy, I told her of the dance spots where my pals and I hung out. As I was trying to be cool, she laughed and said that will do for now.

Naïve as I was, I still didn't realize what she did for a living. When we reached the hotel, she winked and asked what time I got off work, because she would like to help me get off! Like a nervous nerd, I said, "11:00 P.M., ma'am." She registered and I showed Cha-Cha to her room. As I was leaving her room, she gave me a warm, passionate kiss and said, "Chance, don't forget our date." I was breathless as I floated to the front desk.

By the time I got back, I had a special room service request for the presidential suite. This had to be special for me because I knew this meant a very large gratuity. Jorge, the front office manager, told me it was very important people in the suite. As I approached the suite, I was very nervous. When I knocked on the door, a very large Neanderthal opened the door and said, "Come in, kid." As I looked around the suite, all I saw was "no necks" in thousand-dollar suits with gorgeous half-clothed women. The five men at the large marble table were engaged in a very high-stakes poker game. One dandy gentleman got up and said, "Kid, good to see you."

I must have had a shocked look on my face as I said, "You, too, Mr. Sabitino."

"I like you, kid, and I want you to go get us the best pizza in town and my special scotch," he said. He handed me a hundred-dollar bill!

I snapped to attention and said, "Yes sir."

He turned and said, "He's a good boy. Hurry back, kid."

There was only one place to go for pizza, so I ordered four supreme pizzas from Carmine's. I picked up everything as requested and returned within forty-five minutes. As I knocked and entered the suite, the "gorilla" pointed to where I was to set up the food and booze. While I was setting up, I overheard one of the men say, "It doesn't matter, we have to hit Manny and that's it!" Speaking of being nervous as a two bit hooker in church, I was scared. I hesitated a few seconds and said thank you as I handed the change to the bodyguard. Mr. Sabitino jumped up and said, "Keep it, kid, and you finish school, you hear? Thanks, kid."

I said, "Thank you very much," and hurriedly left the room.

After that experience, I went to the men's room to freshen up because I knew I had broken out in a cold sweat. The evening began to get quiet, and I began to get excited about my rendezvous. When eleven o'clock came, I was standing by the time clock. I had always abided by company policies but this one—No fraternizing with the guests—had to be broken! I called Cha-Cha from the house phone and she picked up immediately. I asked if she still wanted to go out. Her sexy voice replied, "Absolutely, you cute thing." I told her where to meet me in the parking lot. I was cocky because with the great tips I had just bought a new yellow Pontiac convertible. Cha-Cha was impressed, too.

Since it was Friday night, I knew that all my friends would be at the Star Light Lounge. When we walked in the lounge, everyone stared at Cha-Cha. Her long dark hair was across one of her large, firm breasts with her inviting dark eyes sparkling as the discotheque lights reflected off of her beautiful face. She was dressed in a short, tight, red, low-cut dress with matching high-heeled shoes. Yes, I felt "hot" just being with her.

My buddies and my ex-girlfriend were there. How sweet it was! I ordered two whisky sours, and my buds came over with their mouths open. I introduced them and immediately we strutted onto the dance floor and continued to show off. She was hot! As the evening progressed Cha-Cha turned out to be as sweet as she was sexy. After a few hours, she suggested we call it a night. While driving back to the hotel, Cha-Cha slid over close to me and began kissing my neck, face, and ear while she was feeling my thigh. When we arrived at the hotel, I was unable to get out of the car immediately.

We made a mad dash to her room. Cha-Cha took charge. She told me to get comfortable as she went into the bathroom. I slipped off my shoes, opened another button on my shirt and mixed us a drink. Wow! Cha-Cha came out in the sexiest black lace bra and panties. My heart began to race as she walked toward me. She took me by the hand and led me to the bed. She began kissing me as she did in the car while continuing to unbutton my shirt. She tossed my shirt across the room. She then began unzipping my trousers. Cha-Cha began breathing passionately and rapidly as she kissed me like I had never experienced. Her big, juicy red lips were all over me as her soft hands touched me everywhere. I had never felt this way in twenty-one years. Cha-Cha looked up and said, "A virgin?" Of course I said no. She said, "I'll know." I had never experienced this kind of treatment by a woman. Wow! Afterwards we went to sleep.

In the morning hours, I felt Cha-Cha kissing me again. Before I could move, she was on top of me. We did the morning horizontal Cha-Cha. Before I left, we talked and I found out what she meant by "Where's the action?" She was talking about a commercial hotel to use her talent as a call girl. It broke my heart, but I told her this was the place. She joined Luís's stable. This naïve All-American boy was getting an education that just wasn't taught in college. At the University of South Florida, I was learning about how to run a business by the book. At the hotel, I learned the facts about the real world.

Two days after I overheard the conversation in the presidential suite, I happened to pick up a *Tampa Tribune* newspaper and on the front was a picture of a slain Manny Garcia. He was shot to death in a famous Ybor City restaurant where known mobsters regularly hung their hats. I knew nothing. I did not share any of my knowledge with my mom, dad, sister, or any of my best friends. I assumed that the men in the suite thought that I did not hear them. Nothing had been said at the hotel and the staff appeared normal. Two weeks passed and I saw Mr. Sabitino come in the lobby. He nodded to me and headed toward the lounge. I smiled back with a sigh of relief and felt a little more relaxed. As time passed, I never heard or read about the murder being solved.

This occupation was quite different from my previous grocery store job. At times hotel work is fast and fun. Then at other times it can be very frustrating dealing with the demanding public. The old saying that the "guest is always right" is definitely not true! One evening as I was being trained at the front office as a front desk clerk, I met my first guest from hell! In my most gracious Southern accent I said, "Good evening, ma'am. Welcome to the Tahitian Hotel and Resort, may I help you?"

She snapped, "A room you ninny."

I said, "Ma'am do you have a reservation?"

"I certainly do!"

"What's the name, ma'am?"

"Mr. and Mrs. Schwartz from New York!"

I began to search for their reservation. No luck! "Ma'am, I don't seem to find your reservation." I inquired, "Are you sure it was for this hotel and for today?" Oh my, that was the wrong thing to ask.

The blue-haired little lady let me have it. "Do you think that I do not know where I am and what day it is?"

"Oh, no, ma'am." She continued, "Get me someone that knows what they are doing and right now. Where's your boss?"

Charles came to my rescue and firmly said, "Mrs. Schwartz, this young man is in training and is doing fine! While you were speaking harshly to Chance, I searched for your reservation also without success." Before she started up again, Charles said, "We have you a lovely poolside room."

She said, "That will not do, because that will be too noisy."

I said, "We have a nice quiet room on the second floor."

Again she said, "No, because the mister can't walk far."

"Ma'am, we have elevators."

She said, "I'm talking to Charles, sonny."

Charles said, "We are almost sold out, but I do have one ground floor room in the back building."

She said, "I guess that will have to do." Mr. Schwartz just smiled and shrugged his shoulders. Mrs. Schwartz continued by asking for any discount tickets for the area. As she registered, she insisted on a senior discount.

I called for a "front." She informed me that they did not need any help. As they left, Charles looked over to me and said, "What a bitch." He said, "Chance, that's not the last we will hear from her."

A few minutes later, the phone rang. "Good evening, front desk, may I help you?" I noticed that the call was from 147. Guess who? "Yes, Mrs. Schwartz, what may I do for you?"

She said, "This won't do, we need two beds."

"Ma'am, that is the last room in the hotel except the other two that you refused."

She said, "Fine, then I need a rollaway, four pillows, and some ice."

I told her that it would be an additional charge of three dollars for the rollaway. She blew her top and wanted to speak to the manager. I patched the call through to Charles. We would never bother Mr. Levine, the general manager, for something like this. Charles firmly said, "Mrs. Schwartz, I found your registration and it has tomorrow's date of arrival, and yes, the rollaway charge will be charged to your room. Jolly is on the way to your room with your requests. Have a nice evening and good night." Charles handled himself professionally with his Spanish charm and accent. About thirty minutes later, another call from 147—"Our air conditioning is not working." I explained the instructions posted at the unit to no avail. I sent Jolly to the rescue. He said, "No way. She stiffed me when I took the rollaway, pillows, and ice." Charles sent Jolly back to assist the guest. The AC worked fine. Jolly was hot, no tip again.

When we came to work the next evening, the front desk staff told us about our favorite guest. She caused a commotion at breakfast. Her eggs weren't cooked properly and the service was too slow. She slipped on the way out of the restaurant. Next, she wanted a completely free stay. That's when Mr. Levine got involved. He apologized, gave the hotel attorney's business card to her, and politely smiled and asked her to stay at the Holiday Inn the next time she was in the area. I liked his style. When the executive housekeeper made her inspections, she reported two sets of towels, two pillows, and all the ashtrays missing from Room 147. Surprise!

As 1961 and 1962 passed, the first American was in space, Marilyn Monroe died, JFK was working on the Bay of Pigs disaster, Jackie was giving a TV tour of the White House and John Glenn orbited the Earth in Friendship 7. With Vietnam heating up, demonstrations began in the streets and on campuses, Joey Dee and the Starlighters were doing the Peppermint Twist. Johnny Carson became the host on the *Tonight Show* and *Lawrence of Arabia* won the best picture of the year. Bermuda shorts arrived on the scene, as did the first hippies and coffeehouses. It was a good year for Jolly and me. Free love was everywhere, and paid love was on call.

Jolly and I were having a good time, making money and getting laid. What else did a twenty-one-year-old college boy need? Better grades! At that time, the hotel and good times had taken over our lives, which we didn't realize at the time. I felt that I was getting an on-the-job education. The hotel general manager had selected me for his cross-training program. I felt honored and privileged while my fellow coworkers called me a brown-noser. I didn't care because I had decided that the hospitality business would be my career. I was trained as a bellman, front desk clerk, night auditor, busboy, and waiter. Of course, I preferred the tipped jobs because of the cash flow. I dropped the idea of being an attorney, CPA, or FBI agent in favor of business courses and all related subjects on hospitality. Instead of being just a job as all the other employees felt, I tried to learn as much as possible, because I knew that I was destined to become an innkeeper. I found this business so interesting because every day was different.

One humid Thursday evening, Cha-Cha called me while I was working and asked me to go dancing. Of course, my active hormones would not resist her, but I told her that Jolly and I had plans. She said fine, we all can party. We strutted into the Oasis Lounge as if we owned it because we knew we were cool. We found a small table near the dance floor and ordered drinks. Cha-Cha and I hit the dance floor as everyone began to stare at us. When we went back to the wafer-sized table, Jolly had spotted a gorgeous blonde at the bar and left us alone. We were having a great time as we watched Mr. Cool work. In a few minutes, Jolly knocked the blonde over a row of tables and chairs. The bouncer and bartenders jumped Jolly, so Cha-Cha and I jumped them. After a good scuffle, we were thrown out as the police arrived. We jumped in the Pontiac and peeled rubber. We had a few bumps and scratches but were laughing as we headed down Dale Mabry Highway.

I said, "Jolly, why in the world did you knock the blonde out?"

He replied excitedly, "Hell, man, that broad was a man!"

"What?"

"You saw me, I was kissing her on the neck as she led me on. Next he put my hand on his crotch and his pecker was bigger than mine!" Cha-Cha and I could not stop laughing. I dropped Jolly at his car and I went over to Cha-Cha's for some more lessons of the world.

As the new year of 1963 came on, the country was experiencing major changes in our way of life, the two most contrasting decades being one before the other. The fifties were a very conservative time with a balanced, respectful, family way of life; the sixties were just the opposite—radical, disrespectful, and wild. My pals and I were caught up in the fast, free, capitalist swinging life.

The hotel was enjoying an 80 percent occupancy with all walks of life coming in and going out its doors. Everyone appeared to be doing fine until the manager, Mr. Levine, disappeared. Upon arriving at work, the rumors were flying. Another thing I had learned, hotels are full of juicy rumors. Mr. Levine's secretary, Silvia, was in tears and very upset. She was a beautifully tailored, sleek young woman who was always sweet to me. Silvia told me that Mr. Levine had been mugged and robbed and that she was going to the hospital. When she arrived, Mrs. Levine and their children were there. As rumor had it, quite a scene took place at the hospital. As I headed to the front desk, a distinguished, well-dressed gentleman said, "Young man."

I said, "Yes, sir, may I help you?"

He introduced himself as the new general manager, Mr. Rossi. He said, "I understand that you are in the cross training program."

"Yes, sir."

"Keep up the good work and keep your nose clean," he replied as he walked toward his office.

Later that evening, in comes strutting Mr. Sabitino. "Hey kid, park my wheels." He tossed his keys and stopped me. He asked if I had met the new innkeeper. Before I could answer, he informed me that no one should become a partner without being invited. He said, "You know what I mean, kid? You're a good kid, keep your nose clean," he told me as he headed toward the lounge. That's twice the same night I heard the same advice. I knew the score.

I got a call from one of the suites for room service. Suite 212 called for some ice, an extra pillow, and a bottle of Cutty Sark. As I opened the door with the requested items, I was daydreaming and did not knock as required with the announcement of "Room Service." I used my master key to enter, and to my surprise, Silvia was doing one of the owners, Mr. Maggiore. They did not notice that I had entered the suite, so I backed out very quietly and eased the door shut. I took a walk around the buildings not noticing that the ice was melting on this humid night. Of course, I was sweating bullets as big as gator tears. My thoughts were running wild. I could have gotten my fingers broken. Was Silvia doing the owner and the general manager? What really happened to Mr. Levine? Oh well, I got myself together and returned to deliver the room service. I knocked and announced very loud, "Room Service." The door cracked and a rough, low voice said, "Come in." The light was low. The gentleman pointed to the table and said, "Put them over there." Mr. Maggiore reached in his robe pocket and handed me a fifty and said, "Keep the change, kid." I sincerely said, "Thank you, sir," and swiftly left the room. Silvia must have been in the bathroom. As I drove home that evening, I thought I had it figured out. Mr. Levine was skimming as well as doing one of the owner's girlfriends. So Mr. Levine wasn't mugged, he was taught a lesson and fired, but at least he was alive. Wow!

The new general manager was quiet, but appeared fair. I did learn from him. Mr. Rossi was in early, greeted the guests, and encouraged all the staff members. In the afternoon, he inspected rooms. As I was trailing Mr. Rossi, he stopped and talked with Ms. Sarah, a great housekeeper. He inspected one of her rooms and found one hair in the bathroom. She was upset and apologized. Then with a little smile, she said, "Mr. Rossi, would you book only bald-headed men into my section?"

We laughed and he said, "Not a bad idea."

The hotel also had a contract with World Airlines for their crews. They were demanding guests with the lowest rates. We had to operate shuttle service to and from the airport upon their request with seldom a tip or a thank-you. Another thing that I never understood was why airline employees received a 50 percent discount while they were traveling and hotel personnel did not receive any discounts when they flew. When Jolly and I heard the hotel had the contract, we thought, "airline stewardesses!" We found out quickly that we didn't have a chance because they were with the pilots.

I did enjoy working with the public because they absolutely amazed me with their impatience. One evening I was at the bell stand and was watching the elevators. We had a large convention group staying in the hotel for a couple of days. A small crowd was waiting for an elevator car. Hardly before the doors opened, a couple of pushy people tried to enter into the crowded elevator before it emptied. I began to wonder why we have such impatient, rude people in our society? Remember, you inconsiderate and pushy people, those on first are the last to leave the elevator car. Overall, as I began to observe the general public, the majority of people are polite and considerate, but a small percentage of our society can ruin your day. One thing about the hippies, they loved everyone.

After watching the charitable, fun-loving Shriners in the Annual Gasparilla Parade each February, I found out the wonderful work they did for the unfortunate children. Then I saw the other side of these pillars of the community. The sales department had booked the state convention for the Shriners with the hotel as its headquarters. They absolutely took over the property. I had never seen so much liquor. Each unit—the band, the clowns, the horse patrol, the motorcycle squad, the scooters—set up hospitality suites. These gentlemen came from all walks of life—businessmen, attorneys, doctors, bankers, merchants, farmers, ranchers, retirees, teachers, ministers, etc. They were big spenders and a hell of a lot of fun.

After their parade, they all rolled back to the hotel. And I mean rolled into the hotel lobby on their Cushman scooters. Three "wild old men" came through the lobby, down the hall, and out the back doors to the pool area. The tiki bar was three deep, chugging down everything in sight while looking at the bartender's big boobs. The area was jammed as these guys made their way around the pool while the crowd cheered them. Then within a split second, two of these old farts drove into the swimming pool. These guys were laughing while security and I pulled them out. Of course, the pool was closed as the two little cycles lay on the bottom. Everyone was hysterically laughing and continuing to party. This group was a fun bunch! In the three days that they were at the hotel, they left a great deal of tips! God bless the Shriners!

Jolly and I were having a good time and making money as we both dropped to part-time students. Jolly had joined the National Guard, and I received my draft notice in the fall of 1963. This had been a good year with the release of the first James Bond movie, *Dr. No,* Tom Jones's sensual flick; while *American Bandstand, The Ed Sullivan Show, Gunsmoke,* and Jackie Gleason were the center of our lives on television. Elvis, Little Richard, and Jerry Lee were still rocking, and we experienced the Motown sounds of the

Supremes and the Temptations, surfing sounds of the Beach Boys and Jan and Dean, the blues sounds of B.B. King and James Brown, the British invasion of the Beatles and the Rolling Stones, and the harder rock sounds of numerous groups. Pop singers Sinatra, Bennett, Como, Mathis, Martin, Nat "King" Cole, and Andy Williams were still producing hits. What a year for a great variety of music.

As Martin Luther King had a dream, the first woman went into space from Russia, the Great Train Robbery took place in England, and the Green Bay Packers won the NFL Championship. This was an exciting, ever-changing and an adventurous year for everyone. Then on November 22 the United States and the world bowed their heads for a dreadful event. President John F. Kennedy was shot and killed in Dallas, a very sad ending for the year. I boarded the train at the expense of the United States Army with reservations at the Ft. Jackson resort in Columbia, South Carolina.

CHAPTER 2

COCOA BEACH, FLORIDA

1965

After my vacation with the U.S. Army, I stopped in Orlando to visit with a buddy. I picked up an *Orlando Sentinel* to check out the classified ads. The Hilton Hotel Corporation had a display advertisement for numerous positions in Cocoa Beach. I wondered, what in the world was in Cocoa Beach besides Cape Canaveral Space Center? Since I didn't have much of a resume, I decided to drive to the beach and investigate. As I drove through West Cocoa, I thought, what am I doing here? The closer I got to the beach, the nicer it appeared. There was no problem finding the Hilton site on Highway A1A since there was only one main street in town. When I drove into the small beach community, I noticed numerous restaurants, go-go bars, nightclubs, and lots of bikinis. This area may not be so bad after all, if I get the job. When I arrived at the hotel site, the personnel office was in a construction trailer. The hotel was near completion from the outside appearance. I applied for a management trainee's position, which would be in the accounting office. Even though there were hundreds of applicants, I felt good when I left. I felt I had enough college, two good years of experience and part of my military obligation complete.

I headed home to Tampa with high hopes of hearing from the Hilton. It was good to be home to see my family and friends even though things were changing. I told my pals, Jolly and Phil, about this booming area, and they said, "Let's go." About a week passed and I received a call from the Cape Kennedy Hilton. John Dalain, the comptroller, offered me a job as his assistant. I excitedly accepted and would start in a week. I went to the beach early in order to check out the territory and find an apartment. I got lucky immediately and found a cool little bachelor pad on the oceanfront in the south beach area near the world famous Bernard's Surf Restaurant. My landlady was an attractive, older, eccentric lady in a flowing see-through gown. She had a drink in one hand and a long cigarette in a jeweled holder in the other. After hard negotiation of terms, Mrs. Penelope Wheeler, widow of General Nathan Wheeler, offered me a drink. As we sipped our cool Tom Collins and enjoyed the warm afternoon ocean breeze from my new balcony, we began to get acquainted. Again I felt naïve and innocent as I learned of Penelope's worldly travels and experiences. She was a very interesting and intelligent lady. She learned of my short background, smiled, and said, "You're cute." Penelope winked and said, "I'll get us another drink." She was back in a flash and as we continued to chat, she took me by the hand and headed toward the bed. As she began kissing me on the face, I pondered, am I being seduced by a rich, older woman? After a steamy, passionate lovemaking session, Penelope gave me a sweet peck on the lips and said, "Thanks, sweetie! Now, love, get me a cigarette." As I leaped up, I was still weak in the knees. As soon as she finished her fag, she dressed and said she had to go to a dinner party at the Officer's Club on Patrick Air Force Base in honor of the astronauts. She told me that I should get out for the evening. She continued and told me to go to the Vanguard Lounge for their jam session. When she left, I thought, what a crazy woman and a strange, exciting afternoon.

It was early evening as I drove to the lounge by the ocean just off Highway A1A. As I drove down A1A, I noticed numerous night spots—The Cape Colony Inn, Wolfie's, The Pillow Talk Lounge, Johnny's Hideaway, The Missile Lounge, The Continental, The Mousetrap, Ramon's, The Samoa Club, The Caravelle Lounge, The Rainbow Room, The Lamp Post, The Carnival Club, The Gemini Room, many "beer joints," and after-hours clubs. I thought that everyone in these small beachside towns of about 7,500 people must drink all the time! For such a tiny city, every club featured entertainment. This was the happening strip because of the space boom.

As I approached the lounge, the parking lot and streets were full of automobiles. I strutted into the lounge with my pale yellow Palm Beach sport jacket with a black silk shirt and matching slacks. I felt super cool! The joint was packed—three deep at the bar, body to body on the dance floor, while the blues band played "Goin' Up" by Jimmy Reed. There were all walks of life in the place. All ages, men in coats, some in cut-offs, women in miniskirts, jeans, and bikinis. It was a jumping joint. When I made my way to the bar I asked Del, the bartender, if that was Alan Shepard at the end of the bar? He nodded affirmatively. While playing it cool, I leaned against the bar and surveyed the place. This was the first cocktail lounge that I had ever seen with as many women as men—Wow! What a meat market.

I spotted a table with four beautiful ladies. I called Del again to ask who they were. He smiled and said, "They are all friends and are hair dressers. They're cool." One of the ladies was petite, gorgeous, and classy, and before I could get to her, three "Hard Tails" were waiting to dance with her. So I grabbed the tall, attractive blonde and we boogied down. I could see that it was girls' night out and they could not be separated that night. So I got a phone number and asked for an appointment for a hairstyle. Well, at least I met the most beautiful lady in the place. Her name was Jo-Jo Reade and she was from England. After dancing all night I was sweaty as a Kentucky Thoroughbred. I decided to grab some breakfast at the Dobbs House before going home to my new pad.

I called Jolly and Phil to tell them about Cocoa Beach. Phil was on his way the next day. The week before going to work, we cruised up and down the beach during the day, met women and partied at night. Jobs were plentiful at the Cape and throughout the hospitality industry. Phil landed a job immediately at the Cape as a welder working on the Vehicular Assembly Building (VAB). Jolly came over by the end of the week. All of a sudden I had two roommates. We struggled for a while in my one-bedroom until we moved into a new two-bedroom apartment at the swinging Wakulla Apartments. Every weekend there was a pool party with all the in crowd. On the first Sunday, I spotted that gorgeous little British beauty in her red polka-dot bikini by the pool. We exchanged eye contact and smiles. She was surrounded as usual.

I laid out the house rules, responsibilities, and the light system. The light system was set up for when one of us was entertaining a lady: the outside light would be left on. Of course, Jolly had to put in a red bulb. Speaking of Jolly—with all the jobs around, our pal didn't find a job for a while. Jolly was happy-go-lucky, a hell of a lot of fun, and he would always survive. One evening, he brought home two ten-pound sticks of bologna. Of course Phil and I asked, "Where did you get them?"

Jolly laughed and said, "It was a miracle. They just rolled out of the back of the meat truck when it stopped at the Crossway Inn." It came in handy since Phil and I hadn't been paid yet. We learned to prepare bologna twenty different ways—fried, baked, sautéed, boiled, cold, etc.

Jolly stumbled on another scheme while reading *The Today* newspaper. He saw rewards for lost dogs from wealthy people. As Jolly strolled the beach carrying bologna strips, he "found" cute little poodles and other spoiled canines. At one time when I came home, we had three precious little "lost" dogs. Jolly would return the pets, collect the one hundred dollars or more, and we would celebrate. Jolly finally found a real job as assistant restaurant manager at the Sheraton Cape Colony. Phil and I did not know how Jolly swung that job, but he had a great personality and a line of BS.

I dressed in my new three-piece Wolf Brothers suit and reported to John Dalain at the Hilton. I was excited as I continued on my pathway to becoming an innkeeper. Joe introduced me to the general manager, the executive assistant, and the rest of the staff. Most were dressed in golf shirts. John showed me around the property, which was due to open in thirty days. We finished the paperwork, and John handed me a list known as a construction punch list. For the next thirty days we reviewed punch lists, checked furniture, processed invoices and payroll, all other accounting functions and anything else that needed to be done. Mr. Gailey, the GM, told everyone at every staff meeting that he never wanted to hear anyone on his staff say, "It's not my job."

While the general contractor, architect, and designers were fighting to finish, the staff was rushing to set up the front desk, the executive offices and each department—sales, catering, housekeeping, laundry, maintenance, food, beverage, and all their inventories. We all worked as an efficient team and were prepared for a spectacular grand opening. The Cape Kennedy Hilton was readied to receive its invited guests. All staff members were reminded to be in formal wear or their designated new colorful uniforms. We all stood tall as the owners, VIP guests, and Mr. Hilton arrived. Mr. Simpson (owner representative) and Mr. Hilton cut the very large red ribbon to officially open this beautiful Mediterranean-designed hotel. Specially prepared food of a great variety featuring elaborate ice carvings and cocktail bars were throughout the entire public areas. Live entertainment in the lounge and a swinging combo by poolside set an upbeat, festive atmosphere. This is the fun part of the business—a spectacular opening that I had the privilege to enjoy and take the opportunity to socialize with the guests. Tomorrow will be different—back to a regular hard-working schedule and no fraternization with the guests!

The hotel was an instant success, being the closest inn to the Kennedy Space Center. We became the in spot where the astronauts, visiting dignitaries, and celebrities stayed while in town. Of course with the Hilton reputation, the general public wanted to rub elbows with the rich and famous.

As time passed, the owner's representative became more difficult to deal with each day. He was at the hotel every day, consistently criticizing the management of the property. Being an upcoming junior executive, I had to become a politician—loyal to the Hilton Hotel Corporation and honest with the ownership. The property was owned by the Southern Development Company, franchised and managed by The Hilton Hotel Corporation. Hilton did exceed budget in the category known as the House Account. We had everyone from Hilton Corporate coming and going. A vice president of operations, a VP of sales and marketing, a VP of food and beverage, a VP of public relations, director of maintenance and housekeeping, relatives, corporate clients, and others were abusing complimentary rooms, food and beverage privileges, as well as telephone and other expenses. Being in accounting, I could see both sides of the conflict.

After two years and many debates, the Hilton Hotel Corporation agreed to terminate the management contract. Mr. Phillip Simpson, the vice president of The Southern Development Company, assumed the responsibility of management. Since this property was one of the first franchised Hilton Inns and successful, the big "H" sign remained. The key corporate staff was transferred to other company properties. Mr. Dalain offered me a position with him at the Boston Hilton Hotel. I spoke with the rest of the staff as well as Mr. Simpson. I was still pursuing Miss Jo-Jo Reade and enjoying the beach life. I stayed with the local ownership and received a promotion and a raise! Since I was the youngest staff member, I was scheduled as the Manager On Duty (MOD) when everyone else wanted off. That was okay because Mr. Simpson began to notice.

At the time, I did not realize that Mr. Simpson and his girlfriend, Marilyn Moore, were using me as their spy. Mr. Simpson appointed Marilyn as public relations director—in other words, in everyone's business. One thing for sure, he had good taste in women. Marilyn was a sleek, tall, beautiful blonde in her early thirties. He was in his mid-fifties, tall, thin, and rich. Mr. S. was also very thrifty, arrogant, egotistical, intelligent, and at times very cruel and physical. On a few occasions, I had to separate Mr. S.'s hands from Marilyn's throat. One other item, he was extremely jealous! Besides being very attractive, Marilyn was very flirtatious. While Mr. S. was out of town, Marilyn acted as if she ran the hotel as well as having her choice of men. I witnessed her leaving the Palms Lounge with an astronaut, a musician, and a politician, as well as Terry Waters, a local lover boy. A few months later, the lover boy was on the hotel sales staff. Strange enough, Terry and I became good friends. One evening, Marilyn made a move on me, but I excused myself and made an exit through the kitchen. I knew not to dip my pen in the inkwell that signed my paycheck.

We had three general managers within a year and a half since the local takeover. The first, Mr. Paul Garbo, resigned; the second, Mr. Joe Graza, was fired; and my favorite, Mr.

Max Meyers, told Mr. S. and Marilyn what to do with their hotel and went back to a four-star property. They drove every innkeeper crazy.

Mr. S. was difficult with everyone except me. Of course, I worked hard, kept my mouth shut, and did my job. Now as the comptroller, I had to keep every department in check. My accounting department handled personnel, payroll, inventories, controls, policies and procedures, and all accounting functions and responsibilities including the financial statements and taxes. Of course, Mr. S. had to try to tell me how to expense line items for tax purposes. As Mr. S. was running the hotel, I advised him that there was a serious rumor throughout the hotel—union talk!

"Damn them," was Mr. S.'s response. "I have been very good to the employees—first I gave them a job with good pay and benefits. The ungrateful bastards!" The salaries and wages were fair but the benefits were not great.

Late one evening as I was working on the books, Mr. S. walked in and asked me to step into his office. I thought, "Oh well, what the hell." Very politely, he told me to have a seat and asked what I would like to drink. He sent Marilyn for cocktails. As he stared with his cold gray eyes into mine, he asked me what we should do about the situation and what would I do if I managed the property. I thought for a moment and my first response was, "Mr. S., we are in the hospitality business and we must develop a staff of smiling, happy people creating a friendly atmosphere for our guests." I continued by saying that I would get aggressive and get all the business in town. I held my breath.

As Marilyn and Jamie (our blonde bombshell cocktail waitress) entered the office with the drinks, Mr. S. snapped, "Do you know how to knock?" They apologized, sat the drinks down, and left. He looked at me with a cheekish smile and said, "Congratulations, Mr. General Manager."

I went silent in shock. I hesitated and said, "Let me think about it." He then looked shocked because Mr. S. always got his way and didn't take "No" for an answer. I smiled and said, "How much?"

He put up his glass and said, "Enough, because I like your style." We worked late into the night developing a plan for the hotel. Mr. S. was making the announcement the following day and then leaving on a business trip. He expected me to put an end to the union organizing. I was thrilled getting the position and being the youngest hotel manager, twenty-seven years old, with the Hilton Hotel organization. I was also scared to death facing the challenges ahead.

Mr. Simpson called a staff meeting and introduced me as the new innkeeper. As I looked around the room, the high-powered department heads' faces were in awe—especially Clive Lawson, chief engineer. Clive was the ringleader in favor of a union. While Mr. S. was laying down the law, everyone was whispering. Everyone was older than me, so I knew I was going to get a hard time. Mr. S. slammed his fist on the podium and everyone got silent. He said, "I expect everyone to cooperate with Mr. Chance Wayne while other changes will be taking place. If you aren't happy working here, you can hit the door now!" All was quiet as no one left. The meeting adjourned. Mr. S. left briskly while some of the staff offered me congratulations.

I called Jo-Jo at her beauty salon and asked her to meet me at the Mousetrap for a drink. She was hesitant but agreed. I called Phil and his new girlfriend, Pam, to meet us. Sadly, Jolly had lost his job and had gone back to Tampa. We celebrated my new position late into the night. Again, I tried to take Jo-Jo to my apartment—again a sweet smile, kiss on the cheek, thanks but not tonight. She was always such a lady—I guess it was her proper English upbringing. Jo-Jo was a gorgeous, petite blonde with a beautiful broad smile, a curvy body, and shapely legs. She was also classy and educated, and she owned Josephine's Coiffeurs. This was the swingingest beauty salon anyone had ever seen. The salon had a modern black, white, and silver decor, upbeat music, complimentary refreshments, and a hip staff of twelve in uniform. Jo-Jo created the first unisex shop in the area. All the "night people"—entertainers, bartenders, cocktail waitresses—as well as the "day people"—Cape employees, Jewish princesses, senior swingers, and most of the astronauts' wives—were Jo-Jo's clientele. What a gossip factory!

Even though I had a head the size of a watermelon, I was on my new job at 6:30 A.M., prepared to tighten the place up and show them who's boss. I walked the property and made notes on everything. I reviewed all the paperwork with Gus, the night auditor. He mentioned he had a small problem with the NCR 4200, which we solved together. Gus was a fifty-eight-year-old gentle, quiet man who always showed loyalty to me. Second, I called a department head meeting in which I tried to act like Mr. S. by laying down what is expected from each department. Every department had to meet their budget every month with no exceptions. The food and beverage director, Randolph Dennis, was a very particular, precise, and strange little Englishman. I knew I had his support since I worked close with him on inventories and controls. Hugo Monger, our executive chef, was a huge, arrogant, and loud German, but he ran a tight kitchen and could make me look good. I felt I would have his support even though he did call me "Kid" when we worked together. I wasn't sure about the sales manager, June Winton, because she expected to be promoted to the GM position. Corey Johnson, the front-office manager, would give me her support. The executive housekeeper, Donna Duggan, was a question mark since she and Clive were close. Clive is going to be a problem, since he already had said, "I will not work for a smart-ass, brown-nosing college kid."

Next, I called a general staff meeting to inform everyone what was going on and the plan Mr. S. and I formulated. Marilyn came prancing in and said with authority, "Why wasn't I informed of these meetings?" I said, "Thank you, meeting adjourned." I turned to her and said, "Never speak to me in that manner again! If I thought there was a need for you to be here, I would have called you—that is, if I could find you!"

"Phil told me to keep an eye on things," she responded.

"That's fine, you can spy all you want but do not interfere with the operations of the hotel, period! You understand? Now go do your P.R. stuff because I have to put out some fires you started as well as run a hotel!"

As I visited each department, I could feel friction—the older employees being loyal to the hotel while the newer ones were pushing for a union. In the meeting, I avoided the union subject, but per our plan we added two more paid holidays, sick days, and one free meal per day. We already provided health insurance, paid holidays, and vacations. The union representative was promoting higher wages per job description, full benefits, and a pension plan with the promise of the pie in the sky. The lazy ones were listening, I became worried. Clive was undermining management while he was supposed to be a supervisor. The other line workers listened to Clive because he had been at the property since it opened. Instead of helping and setting an example, he was always bitching and moaning. By Florida law, even though it is a right-to-work state, we could not stop the employees from voting in a union. It was a split house with most from the front of the house including the food and beverage department giving a negative vote while the back of the house voted positive.

While Mr. S. was gone, I kept our corporate attorney close for advice on the union activities. In the meantime, I was trying to implement our plans—hire an administrative assistant/secretary, control the food and beverage costs, stabilize a couple of departments, put pressure on the sales department, create an advertisement program for our new promotions, maximize room revenue, prepare for a Hilton inspection, and shop for bids while installing a purchase request program. Of course with my cocky attitude I thought I could handle everything myself. I was trying to be like Mr. S.—tough! I was, even though I lost a few good employees.

Before Mr. S. returned, the union was voted in—what a mess. Jack Steinburg, our attorney, and the union officials set up a meeting. I thought Mr. S. would be extremely upset but he surprised me. I explained what went on and that I had initiated our plan. He said, "Fine, let's get prepared for our meeting in two weeks."

Finally, I persuaded Jo-Jo to date me on a regular basis. Phil, Pam, Jo-Jo, and I became a regular foursome. I think I won Jo-Jo when we had our second date at the beach on a beautiful Sunday afternoon. I picked up a bucket of Colonel Sanders Chicken, put the top of my car down, and picked up the British beauty. We picked a spot on the beach, threw out the blanket, and set up for the day. As we strolled, hand in hand, in the warm sunshine down the white sandy beach I felt a song coming on. I broke out in my rendition of Bobby Darin's "Mack the Knife" as people watched. I saw her face turn pink and she said in her cute accent, "You are insane, Love."

I said, "Really, maybe you need to join me." I picked her up as I continued to sing. I spun her around and around and put her down. She was dazed, dizzy, and laughing. Three or four older couples were watching us and smiling. We had a great day!

The hotel was experiencing a high occupancy while food and beverage sales increased each week. Even though an undercurrent ran throughout the property, most of my department heads and I continued as if nothing was going on, in order to make our guests feel comfortable.

By the time our meeting with the union arrived, we were prepared. We had the executive board meeting room set up, all the personnel files, needed hotel records, workman comp files, and statistics from our competitors including a wage and salary survey. In comes Tony Damarco, the no-neck union representative with a half-dozen unsavory characters including their slick mouthpiece, Clive; Harriett, a maid; and Joe, a dishwasher. They strolled in puffing on big stogies when Mr. S. jumped up and said, "There is no smoking in this room!" Boy, I could see this was going to be interesting. On our side of the negotiating table were Mr. S., our attorney, and myself. On their side were ten determined-looking people—some looked like gangsters, city slickers or pimps, and rednecks. Everyone was introduced and you could feel the tension.

Mr. Simpson said, "Let's not waste time. What do you want to hold us for?"

Jack, our attorney, put his hand on his forehead. The union spokesman said, "These people have the right and need for representation."

Mr. S. responded, "Why? I built this hotel, built the business, created jobs, and hired all local people. I do not need a bunch of city slickers to tell me what to do for my employees!" He was getting more and more aggressive. Jack was trying to calm him as he whispered in his ear.

Tony came back calmly, "Mr. Simpson, we are here to talk and to compromise." We took a break.

When we came back, we picked up where we left off. Mr. S. had calmed down and let Jack continue with Tony. Tony presented his demands. They were requesting basically the same benefits as federal government employees with a major increase in wages across the board. It didn't take but seconds until Mr. S. jumped up and said, "This is outrageous! We are not the federal government, and we will not be exhorted. Damn you, strike if you want!" We packed our briefcases and left, leaving the gang with their mouths wide open.

We proceeded to the office to formulate a plan. We laid out a new classified ad, printed a flyer to distribute at the colleges, the Space Center, senior center, apartment complexes, and the unemployment office. I told Mr. S. that I should walk the property and visit with the staff. It appeared all was calm and everyone was working as usual. I called Jo-Jo and she was not home. I went to the Lounge to drink with some friends. There were the usual dudes and honeys drinking and dancing. I had customers/friends with names like Cotton, Skipper, Whitey, Ronson, the Houseman, C.J., Casey the Florist, Irish Joe, The Greek, Bob White, Billy Joe—what a wild bunch. There were broads everywhere. I belted down about six Wild Turkeys and began flirting with Jamie to justify everything—Jo-Jo would not sleep with me, and besides she was not home. I was stressed out. I let Jamie leave early, and we headed to to the apartment of astronaut Ace Shannon's part-time girlfriend.

When I arrived at the hotel the next morning, Clive and his followers were carrying their little strike signs. This continued for a few days with no progress. I had replaced everyone on the picket line—about twenty-five people. As time passed, the line began to dwindle. As this happened, out of frustration they began to block cars entering the hotel, for the guests as well as the employees. I advised all the employees to ignore them until someone threw a rock through a window of my new car. I called the sheriff's department, which put a stop to the interfering of business. That evening about 10:00 P.M., someone called and I received a death threat. This went on for over a week. Late one evening as I left work, I heard a loud bang and a bullet struck my back glass. Luckily it missed, that's why this story can be told. I bought a gun from a friend and would go to work early to avoid the idiots. Actually with this happening, our business increased even more. As time passed, so did the picket line and the union threats.

We got back to business with a much improved staff. The promotions—ladies night, live entertainment every night, seventy-nine-cent cocktail hours, drawings and giveaways, a flambé dining room, and packages were generating more business than expected. Cocktail hours, particularly TGIF (Thank God It's Friday—created at the Cape) was so big that we had to put two portable bars in the lobby. At times it seemed as if half the county was there on TGIF. As I mentioned before, the Hilton was where the "sophisticated mob swings," and it was still considered the in place. We were in full swing along with the space program. The United States was in an overpriced, aggressive race with the USSR to be first to reach the moon.

I knew Jo-Jo was the woman I wanted to marry, but I could not stop having affairs—customers, a cocktail waitress, my restaurant manager, and even my secretary. It seemed that getting laid was a natural way of life. The women just kept coming on to me, but I kept thinking of Jo-Jo. I knew that I needed to reevaluate myself and my lifestyle.

Now some of our friends began to get married. Coyle Jones, my bud from Georgia, and Fay got married. Jo-Jo and I along with two other couples went with them on their honeymoon to Miami. Coyle was one of the funniest men that I had ever met. We all went into one of Miami's fanciest steak houses. The little prissy waiter asked Coyle how he would like his steak prepared. Coyle, in his heavy Southern drawl, said, "Break its horns, wipe its ass, and send it into the dining room." Everyone around us laughed, and the waiter dropped his mouth open. The next day we went to the Orange Bowl and saw the Miami Dolphins beat the New York Jets.

When I returned to work on Monday, the sales department was excited. The King family of Texas had booked the convention hall for an elaborate dinner. They thought the guest of honor would be the president of the United States. The staff—sales, food and beverage, chef, and I—met with the family's coordinator, and she gave us a list of what she wanted without mention of price. Fresh seafood and prime beef as entrees, the best variety of wines, baked Alaska, ice carvings, candles, and silver service was planned for the event. Everything had to be first class. This function was planned for July 1969. The banquet and sales department were busy—we had functions almost every day.

One evening, while walking the property, I went back to see Hugo, our executive chef. He had just finished a huge, successful banquet and was kicking back in his office. I know I smelled alcohol on him on several occasions. I said, "Hugo, great job. Have you been drinking?"

With a serious stare, he replied, "Hell, yes. How do you think I get through this rat race? As I told you, Chance, when you got promoted, let me run my kitchen and I'll make you look good." This he did. He continued, "I have never been drunk on the job or the property as some other management staff." He was right, which included me!

I said, "Hugo, pour me a drink." He took a bottle of Jack Daniels out of his drawer and poured us both a drink. "Cheers, and thanks, Hugo."

I walked over to the convention center, which was adjacent to the hotel. I spoke to Cliff, the security guard. The lights were out in the main hall, but I spotted one was on in the service hallway. While checking doors, I pushed in the walk-in cooler door—what a surprise! There was Wanda (Jamie's cousin) on top of Tony (my best waiter), giving him her best strokes.

I shouted, "What the hell are you two doing?" They scrambled to pull up their clothes.

Tony started, "Boss, we . . ."

I stopped him and said, "Get yourselves together and get the hell out of here!"

"Are we fired?" Tony asked.

"I'll let you know. Get out of my sight." After they left, I shook my head and had to laugh under my breath. Now I had to find Cliff and chew his ass out for not securing the building.

My mom and dad had moved from Tampa to Orlando. Pop told me about the Walt Disney Company buying thousands of acres of land in Kissimmee and West Orlando. He told me that there was a lot happening in these quiet conservative communities. Other major corporations were investing heavily in central Florida. If only we knew how big a boom this area would become. The beach area was still booming while we raced the Russians to the moon. The rest of the world began to take notice of the central Florida area.

The hotel began experiencing more celebrities and dignitaries staying with us. We had Walter Cronkite as a regular guest—what a gentleman. Famous writers such as Gene Rodenberry and Martin Cadin were our frequent guests. Martin and I became rather good friends. He was very outspoken and rather arrogant, but I respected and admired him. He was also demanding but he supported the hotel and was a good tipper to my employees. While filming *Marooned* he housed the cast and crew with us. Gregory Peck was another gentleman, as was the quiet David Janssen. It was a real pleasure and treat meeting these men. It was a thrill to arrange a deep-sea fishing trip for them. Hugh O'Brien was rather conceited. My hero, "The Duke," John Wayne, was absolutely great and as big in real life as on the big screen. Beautiful ladies Connie Stevens and Barbara Eden put a ray of sunshine in the hotel. The far-out cast of *Star Trek* visited with us. We provided accommodations for numerous politicians (e.g., President Nixon, President Johnson, Senator Barry Goldwater, Senator Hubert Humphrey) and foreign visitors such as sheiks and princes. We also had our local celebrities such as Murf the Surf. The most famous were usually the nicest. The richest were usually the most demanding. Security was always a problem and nightmare for the staff. When the presidents visited, the Secret Service took over the property. My staff and I pleased most of them.

The most embarrassing moment was in the Flambé Room where Mr. Cary Grant was having dinner. I had invited Jo-Jo to join me and a client with his wife for dinner. Mr. Grant was dining with his party in a quiet corner. Our party was in the center of the room and Mario was our waiter. Mario was an excellent headwaiter but appeared a little nervous that night. I ordered Steak Diane for the party. I noticed that Mario was also waiting Mr. Grant's table. As Mario prepared the sauce, I thought he was using too much flambé. As we were trying to impress the manager of the McDonnell Corporation, Mario lit the sauce and—boom!—the whole side cart caught on fire. We all jumped up. I threw my napkin in my water glass and began beating out the fire. Mario did the same. I smiled and winked at him and made an announcement, "That concludes our fire and dance show." After everything settled down, I bought everyone in the restaurant a drink. I went to Mr. Grant's table, smiled, and asked if he would like Baked Alaska or Cherries Jubilee. He smiled and replied, "Not tonight, old boy, I'm trying to burn off my own calories." He thanked me and I went back to my table. Mario was so embarrassed, but he performed like a trooper. He came over and told me there was a crowd outside in the lobby waiting for Mr. Grant. I told him to advise me when he was ready to leave. Mario did and I advised Mr. Grant of the situation. He again thanked me in his charming manner. I told Mr. Grant that I could sneak him through the kitchen and to his suite. He was grateful and agreed. As he walked through the kitchen, he spoke to everyone and thanked Hugo for a wonderful meal. Mr. Grant made it to his suite unnoticed. What a class act!

My friend and future competitor Johnny Esposito gave me business with the entertainers he promoted in the area. Johnny was a great promoter. We enjoyed the acts and the people—Brook Benton, Frank Sinatra Jr., The Coasters, The

Platters, The Drifters, Joey Dee and The Starliters, and more. The strange Tiny Tim had to have a pinball machine in his suite.

I invited Jo-Jo to meet my mom and dad, and she agreed. As I took her home after dinner, she gave me a kiss and said, "Would you knock me up in the morning about 7:00, love?"

Now I was in shock. I said, "This is sudden but shouldn't we get married first?" She laughed in a shy way and said, "No silly, give me a call and wake me up."

Jo-Jo was so cute with her English sayings. One evening, she met me for a drink when I was down after a hard day. She said, "Love, now keep your pecker up."

I said, "Here at the restaurant?"

"No, silly, that means your chin." Now I was a little embarrassed. My parents loved her as we two opposites were falling in love.

As July approached—the month for the man-on-the-moon shot—the county began to buzz. Three weeks before, a snappy, granite-faced, tall man in a dark suit from the Secret Service contacted me. He informed me that he needed to review the property in detail due to a special guest. Six men arrived in dark government automobiles wearing dark suits and dark glasses. Agent Jack Stern introduced himself as well as the other gentlemen. He proceeded to tell me that they needed the blueprints of the property, the personnel files of the staff, hours of operations, schedules of each department, types of vehicles of staff, reservations for certain dates, what hotel security we had as well as numerous other items and questions.

After they reviewed the hotel layout, they requested a certain block of rooms near the Convention Center.

Basically we (the hotel staff) were left in the dark (typical federal government). I finally put it together. Moon shot, King family banquet, Secret Service equaled former President Johnson or President Nixon. I called a staff meeting and invited Jack to attend. He agreed and informed us that was the tentative plan and there will be several other VIPs in for this special event.

As we planned this function as well as others, business continued to be great. I felt like I was on top of the world. I was working ungodly hours including my drinking time. I tried to justify this by calling it business with Mr. S. and business friends. I began to feel as if I was losing Jo-Jo. I changed for awhile and asked Jo-Jo to marry me. I planned a very romantic evening when I asked her. She said, "Yes."

We had a fun and wonderful time planning our special event. We married on Palm Sunday in April at the First Baptist Church with over 200 people attending. We received over 250 people at the world-famous Mousetrap at our reception. A great time was had by all! Since we both were workaholics, we only took a few days off in Miami Beach for our honeymoon. We stayed at the Fontainebleau Hotel and were honored at our friends' show—The Rhodes Brothers Revue.

We were both movers and shakers of our time. Jo-Jo's beauty salon was the nerve center of gossip for the area. It was busy day and night, and she worked as hard as I did. My hotel was still the in place. Between our busy schedules we bought a beautiful home on Merritt Island. Jo-Jo personally decorated in elegant professional taste and created a home for us. Timing was perfect because Mr. and Mrs. Reade (my mother- and father-in-law) were arriving from England to visit us.

The Secret Service had arrived and basically taken over the hotel. The town was buzzing and excited because within a week, we were launching men to the moon. This little beach community was packed, and all hotels, motels, inns, and apartments were filled as far as Daytona Beach, Orlando, and Vero Beach. At the time we did not realize how spectacular and historical this event would become. Of course we maximized our room rates for a minimum length of stay. At the time, I did not realize that I was practicing what is now known as yield management.

When Apollo XI blasted off from Pad 39-A at the Cape on July 16, the world's eyes were on Astronauts Armstrong, Aldrin, and Collins. The hotel staffs' pride reflected in its guest relations since we were so close to this event. When July 21 arrived and all of the world heard, "That's one small step for man, one giant leap for mankind," indeed Earth did seem united. President Nixon called the feat "the greatest in the history of the world since creation." One would have thought we all landed on the moon. The town went crazy in jubilation. Parties were everywhere, but not greater than at the Hilton.

We had the special VIP function happening in the Convention Center with Secret Service everywhere—around the building, in the building, and on the roof. They had secured that part of the building tight! Barriers had been set up to divide the entrance walkways to the center and the hotel. What a pain in the ass!

Meanwhile back in the hotel, it was rocking. Combo at poolside, tiki bar packed, lobby packed (two bars), and the Palms Lounge was body-to-body as the Mark Wayne Group played late into the night. What an exciting, festive atmosphere! Jo-Jo met me late and we strolled around speaking to everyone. I needed that because earlier I was as nervous as a virgin in a cathouse. All the staff was "stretched out"—the kitchen could not get the food out (Hugo was handling the banquet), so I helped and expedited for awhile. The bartenders were "in the weeds" so I helped there, too. There were just too many people—it was great! At the end of the day, even though everything was a mess, all went well—thank the Lord!

The next day after reviewing the numbers, we set a record in revenue for one day. This beat the figures of the grand opening. I called a staff meeting to thank everyone for a great job and to ask them to keep up the team spirit and the pride in their work. As we had a general discussion, we also noticed that there were no class barriers yesterday. Our guests from all walks of life were rubbing elbows—Cape workers, engineers, taxi drivers, politicians, bartenders, tradespeople, waitresses, bankers, hair dressers, business people, celebrities—Martin Cadin, Alan Shepard, Gene Rodenberry, Hugh O'Brien, Lee Majors Barbara Eden, Larry Hagman, and several others. I then asked, "How were the tips?" Each department head said everyone was very happy. Then I gave each supervisor an envelope with a hundred-dollar bill inside. They smiled and looked puzzled. I told them that the King family's coordinator passed this along because of a super job. It was a thirty-thousand-dollar banquet for the hotel. John, our comptroller, announced that they have already paid for the function and all gratuities will be distributed on the next paycheck. What a happy staff.

Now for getting paid by our federal government, they demand but do not want to pay. The charges for rooms, food, telephone, and laundry for their block of rooms, it took over four months to get paid. It's a shame that the government is not run like a business. They wasted millions of dollars at the Cape. I had a group of men that took hours for lunch and drinks. At times they would flip a coin to see which of them would go back to clock everyone out. On another occasion, Roger the Dodger, a friend who worked for an aeronautics corporation, told me about a $500 screwdriver. He said it looked exactly like a $1.89 Sears screwdriver. Why can't the United States federal government, the largest employer in the country, balance a budget? Why do government employees receive better benefits than other citizens?

As business continued to boom, almost everyone was having an affair. Cocoa Beach and Cape Canaveral were actually a little Sodom and Gomorrah. Astronauts buzzing around in their Corvettes, surfing contests, bikini beach bunny beauty contests, go-go dance clubs, dance contests, regular rocket shots, strip joints, after-hours clubs, top entertainment, and an entertainer as the mayor. This was a wild, exciting time.

Each little town was in competition with one another. At one time our liquor laws allowed us to stay open until 3:00 A.M. Cocoa Beach voted in a 5:00 A.M. closing time. So Cape Canaveral approved staying open twenty-four hours!

These were truly the good old days. Business good, capable and efficient employees, professional staff, appreciative guests, and thankful ownership. More women than I have ever seen and more money than I thought I would ever make. Again, I was going through a phase of the flesh being weak. Also, being influenced by my friends and that old Wild Turkey, I could not resist my secretary, Jamie, or Nina, a regular customer. I always thought it was okay, because Ace Shannon, the astronaut, had his girlfriends.

About a week before he was due to launch for the moon, Ace called me. "Hey, Chance, do you have the Executive Suite open tonight?"

I checked, confirmed, and said, "Yes, but Ace, aren't you in quarantine?"

"Yes, but hell, I may not get back and I won't have any beaver out there," he laughed.

I asked, "Do you want a bottle of Chivas Regal and the usual set-up?"

"Yea, thanks Chance, I owe you."

I told him that I would handle it personally. I set up the suite as requested, put on low lighting and soft jazz. I also left a note asking Ace to take a special medal to the moon with him.

Roger the Dodger and I would have drinks every Friday, and he would keep me posted on what was happening on the Cape. He would tell me about contracts, who's coming and going, planned shots, and the gossip from Hanger S to Merritt Island. He told me about when Hondo Hooper, one of the first spacemen, went to sleep on the Pad. He was ready but the countdown stopped and was delayed thirty minutes. After a successful shot, my friend found an open bottle of liquor stuffed in the couch of the astronaut's trailer. All went well with a successful recovery in the Pacific Ocean.

I had to clean up my act because my new proper British mother- and father-in-law were coming for a visit. Jo-Jo and I had to plan our tight schedules in order to spend time and entertain Mr. and Mrs. Reade. We picked them up at Miami International Airport. We immediately spotted the properly dressed, handsome, distinguished couple. It was a very happy reunion. They were very proud of their little princess and very polite to me. That's why I love the British—their manners. We showed them all of Florida's original attractions: Cypress Gardens, Gatorland, Weeki Wachee Springs, Daytona Beach, Seaquarium, St. Augustine, Miami Beach, and Key West. They were the sweetest and most grateful little couple that I ever met. They were great about our working schedules and extended their stay.

Instead of flying out of Miami back to New York City, we decided to drive and show them some of the country. One benefit with Hilton was complimentary rooms when available. I was amazed when I called the Waldorf-Astoria and booked two rooms for three or four nights. Even though it was late autumn, it was a beautiful drive. As we approached the Big Apple, it began to snow lightly. I apologized while they smiled and said, "We are used to this." Jo-Jo warned me to have plenty of dollar bills ready for tips. By the time we reached our rooms, I tipped the valet for parking the car, the doorman, and the bellman. They had our reservations but the room clerk tried to charge us. We called for the little snappy assistant manager on duty. He corrected the mistake. Even though the rooms were comp, we were disappointed—a small old room with twin beds and no view. I did call and complain and was informed nothing else was available. The parents said everything was lovely.

The next evening we had plans to go to Broadway and see *South Pacific*. While the ladies continued to get ready, Mr. Reade and I strolled through the lobby and had a smoke. A young bellman asked Mr. Reade, as he strolled around with his hands behind his back, "Can I help you, sir?" Mr. Billy Reade calmly in his strong English accent said, "No, son, if I like the place, I'll buy it."

The bellman, with a surprised look, said, "Very good, sir," and hurried away. Mr. Reade winked at me, smiled, and offered me another fag.

As we were sitting in the beautiful, busy lobby, we were watching a situation develop at the front desk. A very well-dressed businessman was trying to check in per his reservation. The clerk informed the guest that the hotel was full and that they had made reservations at the Sheraton just a few minutes away. The gentleman was very calm as he asked the clerk, "Did I not guarantee my room with my American Express card?"

She replied, "Yes, sir."

He continued by saying, "You expect me to go back out into the snow and freezing weather after a horrible plane trip and a miserable taxi ride."

She said, "Sir, the hotel will pay for the taxi and the first night's stay."

The guest calmly said, "No, thanks, that's fine." As we watched, the gentleman went to the men's room. In a few minutes, he came out dressed in pajamas and a robe with suitcase in hand. He proceeded to an out-of-the-way, overstuffed sofa. He laid out his personal items, put his case out of the way, puffed up a pillow, and stretched out. Mr. Reade and I laughed, and it appeared that we were the first to notice him. Finally the front desk saw him and out came the snappy little MOD. He told the guest that he could not sleep there. The guest was still passive and informed the young man that everything was fine. He continued by saying the hotel guaranteed him a room and if he didn't show up that he would have been charged. The young manager called security. The ladies came down and we told them what was happening and that we had to wait to see the outcome. Security was still with the customer as the prissy little manager came back. Now, the guest was putting his items back into his case and the bellman picked it up and off they went. They got on the elevator and went up. As we were leaving, I asked the bellman that we spoke with earlier, what happened? He smiled and informed us that the MOD called the GM and they put the determined guest in the presidential suite. I learned something as an innkeeper—do not overbook or make reservations that you cannot honor! That guest was not going to be walked.

As we left the hotel, I tipped the doorman again for hailing us a taxi. We got lucky with our cabbie. He was American-Polish. He took us straight to the theatre and agreed to pick us up, which he did. He was also very gracious and took us to a famous New York deli. What a perfect evening. We toured the city for the next two days and had an exciting time. We survived New York, sent the parents off to England, and headed back to Florida.

The 1960s were exciting and turbulent and turned our society upside down in a way that history has never seen and will never see again. The year of 1969 closed the decade with an amazing flurry—the upstart New York Jets upset the powerful Baltimore Colts in Super Bowl III, the surprising New York Mets upended the solid Baltimore Orioles in the World Series, the Boston Celtics defeated the Los Angeles Lakers, and the silent majority said goodbye to *The Saturday Evening Post*.

Technology had peaked with men landing on the moon, the globe connected through satellite communications, with 95 percent of all homes in America having at least one television set, while almost 35 percent had two, and color TV was big business. Medical advances and education allowed the average American to live longer than any time in history.

President Nixon proved his political knowledge by signing the Tax Reform Act, reducing personal income taxes, and removing nine million low-income people from tax rolls. He demonstrated his foreign policy ability by returning from a world tour on which he visited Romania, becoming the first president to visit a Communist nation since World War II. We also lost a great American—Dwight D. Eisenhower, general and president.

The decade of free love, flower children, hard rock, and drugs climaxed in New York at Woodstock. The great variety of entertainment continued as Hollywood produced such movies as *Butch Cassidy and the Sundance Kid*, *Easy Rider,* and the winner of the year was *Midnight*

Cowboy. The "Duke," John Wayne, won a well-deserved Academy Award for *True Grit.* And I got married—what a decade and a banner year!

The 1970s began slow compared to the Sixties. After the United States beat the Russians to the moon, it appeared that NASA had slowed the space programs. We at the hotel noticed fewer out-of-state guests while the local companies and local yokels kept us busy. After only a couple years as an innkeeper, you realize that a hotel manager has to wear many hats. Everyone expects so much of you. The ownership requires a healthy profit and a plan to increase next year's business. The guests expect perfection, or they insist on a discount or a free room, meal, or drinks. The employees expect flawless leadership, excellent working conditions, raises, encouragement, schedules that work around their lives, paid holidays, longer vacations, and understanding when they miss or are late for work. At times I feel like a coach, a priest, a baby-sitter, a mother hen, a leader, a follower, a psychologist, a motivator, a public relations expert, a diplomat, a promoter, a planner, a negotiator, a policeman, a teacher, and a principal, and I feel I should always set an example.

The front desk is the nerve center of the hotel. Everything happens there—check in, check out, information, questions, messages, telephone assistance, complaints, and compliments, and it's where the accounting begins. The good front-desk clerk is a very valuable asset to any hotel because of the variety of duties. Most of the time, people in this job are not appreciated by the traveling public and are generally underpaid by the ownership. Normally they are required to be greeters, cashiers, telephone operators, salespeople, public relations people, liars for management/owners, reservationists, very organized, and any other job deemed necessary by management.

The maids (who should be called housekeepers) are also unappreciated by the traveling public. This is a tough job—to clean up after human beings. The hotel must ensure that each room has been cleaned and sanitized for the next guest. At times the hotel had rooms trashed by the guests. Some of the guests think, the maid will clean it up. One thing I did not understand—why did a guest tip a bartender a dollar for a drink (made in seconds) and no tip for the housekeeper (thirty to forty-five minutes to clean a room)?

As I inspected the rooms in the afternoon, I always tried to speak to and show appreciation to my housekeepers. One day while I was on the floor inspecting, I pulled open a night-stand drawer, and I found a pack of cigarettes and a prophylactic next to the Bible. What a world we live in, and if only motel rooms could talk. My curiosity got the best of me. I had always wondered why all hotel/motel rooms have Bibles? The Gideon organization began this wonderful practice in 1908 at the Superior Hotel in Iron Mountain, Montana. This practice has been continued by all the major chains and independent properties. This wonderful group replaces eighty-six Bibles per minute.

Overall, the Hilton Hotel corporation was very professional and organized. They kept the properties well informed with newsletters and flyers. One week I received a report concerning scams. One notice warned us of a man who identifies himself as Anthony Lombardi of New York City. He has exploited Hilton and Holiday Inns down the eastern seaboard—Maryland, Virginia, the Carolinas, and Georgia. He demands refunds after alleging he found mice in his rooms. In one instance, a hotel employee at the brand-new Savannah Hilton reported that the man carried a cage into his room. It appeared that the man was headed to Florida for a free vacation. Sure enough, a man fitting Lombardi's description checked in under the name of Albert Lambert. I called Security immediately and told him to follow the guest and put a surveillance on him and his room. The man went straight to his room. Later, Security spotted him going back to his automobile and retrieving something from the vehicle. It was a small cage. I called the police and they didn't know what to advise me because he had not broken any laws in the city. I met Security at the room and knocked on the door. He answered, and we walked in and I spotted the cage with two small gray mice. I quickly informed the man that we do not allow pets and we do not have mice in our hotel. I asked for his identification and he refused. I asked him to leave, and before he could say anything I told Security to call the Man. He quickly left. I then had Security call the other beach properties and the other Hiltons in the state.

The federal government employees (NASA, Air Force, Navy, and others) continued to stay with us at a discounted rate. While they do not pay full price for their rooms, at times they are the biggest complainers. Why are federal employees tax-exempt and all other citizens have to pay the room taxes? I guess it is our form of government—the double-standard government. Why don't all citizens get free health insurance, early retirement/pensions, all those paid holidays and sick days, etc.? And then their attitudes are another thing! They should be working for the general population instead of doing us favors.

The major contractors for NASA—TWA, McDonnell, Bendix, Lockheed, Martin-Marietta, General Dynamics, Grumman, Boeing, General Electric, Radiation, and several others were excellent clients. They had their own travel departments, which were organized and paid their invoices on time. Now, our federal government was another story. The space program became a rat race for the contractors. Each company had to have lobbyists, an inside track within the political world with money to ensure securing a contract.

Roger would keep me advised, then my sales department and I would entertain the players. We would talk to the decision makers and wine and dine them until we had a housing contract. This basis of business ensured us meeting the nut of the hotel. Since we controlled the market we were fortunate to have the best staff. With all our liquor promotions, I did have a problem with my bar cost. I decided to hire the best bar manager on the beach—Joe Domigas. I went to see Joe at his work and, as usual, he bought me the first drink. I offered him $150 a week plus tips. He said that he needed $175 a week and he would bring me a bar cost under 20 percent. I said $150—he said $175—I said $150—he said $150 and I'll steal only $25 a week. I said, "Deal."

After I left I thought, if someone tells you that he will only steal $25, will he be straight with you or will he steal $100? Joe worked six nights, no days (he played golf during the day), and brought his own following. He lived up to his word and made me look good. Each month, our bar cost was consistently around 19 percent. The entire staff was finally a well-functioning team. The ownership appeared somewhat happy, and the staff stable made my life easier. I took advantage of the situation as I made excuses to Jo-Jo of working late hours. I drank with Mr. S., his friends, my friends, clients, and anyone that boosted my ego. It was so easy to walk to the Lounge, which turned into a habit.

One evening while drinking with a couple of astronauts and Marty Cadin, they told me they were hungry. Even though the dining room was closed, I had to act like a big shot. The kitchen staff was storing items and beginning to clean the areas. I told the evening cook, Tyrone, what the boys wanted to eat. He said the kitchen was closed. That's all it took. After drinking for hours, in a very loud voice, I informed this big black man that the damn kitchen is now open!

He said, "No, sir, it's closed!"

I said, "Tyrone, you will prepare these orders or you are fired!" In my drunken state I said a few more off-color statements.

Tyrone ordered me out of the kitchen and headed toward me with a butcher knife. I took a couple of steps backward and reached for a pot. As Tyrone came closer, out of fear, I hit him with the pot very hard. He staggered toward me and fell at my feet. I sobered up fast and called an ambulance. I told the other staff to go about their work and went out front to tell the guys the kitchen was closed and I had to leave. When the medics arrived, I told them he slipped. Tyrone went to Cape Canaveral Hospital and I followed. I told the emergency room we would take care of all expenses. Doctor Weinburger decided to keep him overnight for observation. Thank God it was only a slight concussion. Early the next morning, I called the hospital to check on Tyrone. He was fine and was being released. I was waiting to drive him home. I apologized, he accepted, and I gave him a week off with pay. When Big T returned to work, I gave him a raise and a paid vacation at the end of the summer. All turned out well for the hotel and myself. I changed my working habits and went back to basics.

As 1970 was passing very fast, I could see this decade was going to be different from the Sixties. With the deaths of Jimi Hendrix and Janis Joplin, fresh new sounds of The Carpenters, The Jackson Five, The Osmond Brothers, Creedence Clearwater Revival, The Partridges, and John Denver were changing the music scene. Exceptional films such as *Patton* and *M.A.S.H.* opened the Seventies with record crowds at the movies.

As 1970 came to a close, rumors were floating around town that the hotel was being sold. Business continued to be very good compared to our competitors. We did notice a slight slowdown at the Cape. Mr. S. would come by the hotel early each morning, and I noticed that it appeared he was avoiding me. He was not in the cocktail lounge as often as in the past. Mr. S. sent his right-hand man, George Freeman, to meet with me to review hotel operations. One day George came by and we had lunch, and he made reservations for a block of complimentary rooms for visitors from Cape May, New Jersey. George and I became close friends. He did tell me that Mr. Simpson had been in secret closed-door meetings and that he had not been invited.

A week before these guests were to arrive, Mr. S. finally met with me. At that time, he informed me that Southern Development Corporation was selling the property to Dr. Carl McIntire's organization. I must have looked in total shock as I asked, "Who's Carl McIntire?"

Mr. S. told me that in his master business plan, he sells when business is on top, not the bottom. He said that he was selling the apartment complexes as well as the office buildings across the street. He continued by telling me that Dr. McIntire is a media minister and that he owns hotels, radio stations, a college, and various real estate holdings. Mr. S. told me that McIntire had a massive following, particularly in the senior market. Mr. S. asked me to inform the staff and treat the tentative new owners as VIPs. Telling the staff the sad news was the most difficult task that I'd had to face since I had been in the hospitality industry.

Upon the day of arrival of the tentative new owners, I was pacing in the lobby as three black limousines pulled up in front of the hotel. My staff and I greeted Dr. McIntire and his entourage. They were pleasant but rather cold and all business. While they wandered around the property asking questions, everyone was nervous about losing their jobs. The warm, happy atmosphere turned to a strange, uneasy environment. Mr. S. announced that the new owners would take over in seventy-two hours. Gary Graham, McIntire's vice president, met with me to plan the changeover. He offered me a job to join their organization. Gary asked me to speak to the staff. I agreed.

I formulated a plan to close out the night audit, cut off accounts receivable and payable, payroll, and inventories. Gary presented his plan: Close the lounge, terminate the beverage department, lay off half the food staff, review functions/banquets and cancel any with liquor, scale down housekeeping and maintenance, and cut sales and front-office staff. I immediately had a resumé typed, and I advised everyone to do the same. I asked Mr. S. what to do with the food and beverage inventories. He replied, "Get as much as you can." So I planned a party for our employees and our regular clientele.

We closed the hotel as strong as we opened. This was a very sad day for the area and all concerned. The party began exactly at 4:00 P.M. when the cocktail hour opened. I had two bands lined up, drinks at seventy-nine cents, and at 11:00 P.M. we began auctioning all the booze. The place was swinging, the dance floor packed, everyone hitting on everyone, and I was peddling booze. What a night to remember.

The next day was very strange. I was instructed to lock the entrances to the lounge, remove all ashtrays from the property, order a variety of signs, remove the tiki bar, meet with all employees to find out who was staying, and set up a meeting with Hilton officials. Gary informed me the new name of the hotel would be Gateway to the Stars. Their major source of revenue will be the bus business. With this strange business plan, I finished my obligation to Mr. S. and resigned. I had no regrets; it had been a good six years. I was surprised, disappointed, hurt, and simply did not understand. The hardest part of the whole thing was telling

Jo-Jo. As usual, she was understanding, supportive, and very comforting to me.

This appeared to be the end of an exciting, unique era in history. The original seven astronauts were partners with Mr. Henry Landsworth (a great hotelier), owner of The Cape Colony Inn. They did have the "right stuff" going through the Mercury, Gemini, and Apollo space programs and winning the race to the moon. To me it was the end of the space program after meeting the original seven and the second group of space men that walked on the moon—Neil Armstrong, Buzz Aldrin, Pete Conrad, Alan Bean, Edgar Mitchell, Dave Scott, James Irwin, John Young, Charles Duke, Eugene Cernan, Harrison Schmitt, and my pal Alan Shepard. Alan made the longest golf shot in history with a 6-iron when he made his visit to the lunar surface in 1971. After six trips to the desolate heavenly body, the Apollo program ended, as did a great hotel. A sleepy beachside town became a boomtown while entertaining celebrities and world figures. The area began to be somewhat more stable and not as exciting.

Before Jo-Jo and I could plan a vacation, I had three offers of employment and opportunities. Of course they all were counting on me to bring the in crowd and increase their business. The Sheraton Cape Colony and the Ramada Inn offered me the innkeeper's positions while Vic Valentini offered a partnership. Vic had quite a reputation, as did his senior partner, the wealthy, eccentric Cecil D. Buford. Jo-Jo knew of these characters and advised me not to go into business with them. They made me an offer that I couldn't refuse—25 percent ownership of The Red Carpet Caravelle Motel and Lounge. I had an agreement drawn up by Jack Steinburg giving me 25 percent of the property, which had one hundred units and a cocktail lounge that seated 125 persons. It was also on the water with a swimming pool. The motel was in poor condition (it sure wasn't a Hilton), and the bar was nice but closed. This was going to be a challenge, but I felt I could make it successful by bringing in the Hilton clientele.

I called a meeting with my new partners to formulate a business plan. They told me to do it—Cecil said that he is the silent partner because he doesn't work! He would meet with us when needed. Cecil could always be found around lunchtime (martini lunches) at Ramon's just down the street. Vic would oversee the motel housekeeping and maintenance. My direct responsibilities included the accounting, the lounge, and the sales and marketing. I asked Vic to clean up the property, and he agreed. I concentrated on opening the Caravelle Lounge. We were losing money each day it stayed closed, especially me. My agreement called for 10 percent of gross income. We worked around the clock to prepare for a Grand Re-Opening. We had to open with a bang—new promotions, a good band, and a staff with personalities—because the competition was very tough.

The little town still had top entertainers—The Carnival Club starred Lee Caron and The Sharpshooters, Johnny's Hideout had Bobby Cash and The Night Flyers, Cape Colony Inn featured The Mark Wayne Revue, as all clubs continued with hot bands. This was tough enough but other new clubs—The Shark Lounge and The Anchor Club—were opening. I called several booking agents, and we decided to open with The Sunshine Band from Miami, to be followed by The Jaguars. All was ready—four experienced bartenders, six beautiful cocktail waitresses, advertisements in place, and everything set up. We had an exciting Grand Opening with a much larger crowd than expected. Vic and I both were out front greeting everyone and working the crowd. We continued through the weekend and climaxed with a bikini contest, a pool party, a Bar-B-Q, and a live radio broadcast. We were contacted by the local police department about the traffic problem, so we hired a couple of policemen to handle the traffic. Vic and Cecil were surprised at the turnout, but I had felt we would do well. I had spoken with some of the main players from the Hilton, and word of mouth spread. Jo-Jo helped promote through her beauty salon and the loyalty of our friends. As sunset came over the Banana River, the outside activities were coming to a close. We moved the festivities inside. I had been Master of Ceremonies for the day and thoroughly enjoyed the job. While walking back to the office, Ginger, the beautiful little redhead who had won the bikini contest, said that she would like to thank me for the prize. I smiled and said, "That's nice but I have to go to the office." She followed. I sent her to get us a drink as I made the cash drop from the pool bar. She knocked on the door with the drinks in her hands. I opened the door and asked Ginger to have a seat. We lit up a cigarette and I sat down on the couch with her. Her firm, stacked little body was still in an orange polka-dot bikini. I thought, "I should not be here." As she worked her little foot up my pants leg, I began to get aroused. I grabbed her by the neck and gave her a kiss and she responded by straddling me. She thanked me for the one-hundred-dollar prize in a very exciting way! Vic knocked on the door and I said, "Just a moment." Ginger left to get her clothes from her car. Vic laughed and we went to the Lounge for another drink. I got home a little late and told Jo-Jo how successful the opening was and how hard I worked. She was sweet and understanding as usual. While laying in bed with the most wonderful woman, I felt guilty and thought that I was getting away from being a hotelier.

While driving to work the next day, I felt proud of taking a closed Lounge and becoming an instant success. When I arrived at the office, Vic was already there. He was always early and did work hard on improving the motel. We reviewed my plan, which primarily concerned promoting the cocktail lounge. To stay ahead of the competition, we must give the public what they wanted and something they didn't. We also had to be bold. We introduced the first free Ladies Night on Mondays (our slowest night). We hired Cotton, a big, good-looking, Southern, blonde local lover boy as the ladies bartender. He had the honeys lined out the door at his bar. We hired John Bugos, a former National Football League tackle as our doorman/bouncer. We contracted top touring bands. We had large TGIFs where anyone who received a pink slip at the Cape would drink free. We promoted jam sessions, talent contests, dance contests, bikini contests, pool parties, holiday parties, balloon party night, or any crazy idea that would sell rooms and liquor.

Vic and I would begin having a cocktail at Happy Hour with our friends, and we would continue all night. When I did M.C. work or sang with the house band, I would have to have another drink for courage. Business was very good as we noticed all walks of life were our clientele. The place rocked as the in place and meat market of the beach. I was having fun with the lounge, but the motel was beginning to worry me.

As competition got tougher, we constantly would have a brainstorming session with Wild Turkey and Dewar's. I contacted Buddy King Promotions in Nashville for some bigger acts. I was getting tired of the attitudes of the road bands. Vic and I began looking for house bands. We promoted our jam sessions to have a look at local musicians. One Sunday, we were sitting at the bar and a new sound caught my ear. I took a look and there were only three guys "putting down some sounds." We started listening as did everyone in the place. They finished playing as another group went to the stage. I called them over for a drink and asked how long have they been together. Bob, the drummer, said about a month. I tried not to show how impressed I was by their music. I asked them to play the closing set. They were elated. While they played, the crowd was into their music and my mind began to work. Vic and I were having a nightcap when it came to me—Black, White, and Ugly. One black dude (keyboards), tall white cat (guitar), and a husky white guy (drums), who could all sing with different styles. We signed them as our house band, dressed them in black and white, and they became an instant hit.

To stay ahead of the competition we installed telephones at all bar stools and tables. At times it would become a crazy, fun madhouse. Everyone was calling everyone and getting lucky. A year later in the Miami area, a company opened several lounges with phones (similar to ours) called "The Phone Booths"—very interesting. All lounges began featuring Ladies Nights. I called Buddy King and we brought acts in such as Jimmy Velvet, Gary US Bonds, Chubby Checker, Jerry Lee, and others. Again, traffic jams in front of the motel.

Vic and I both were drinking excessively, enjoying our friends, and having sleazy affairs with our customers and our staff. This filtered back through Jo-Jo's beauty salon. One evening after not calling home, I went home drunk. A lovely spaghetti dinner was on the table. Jo-Jo came out and asked what I would like to drink. I laughed and said I had enough. She had enough and dumped the plate of spaghetti on my head. First, I got mad. Jo-Jo slammed the bedroom door and I looked at myself in the mirrored wall. As the spaghetti trickled down my velvet suit I had to laugh at myself. Men, take my advice, at least make a telephone call if you are going to be late!

One evening, Bob Bentley's pager went off. He was one of our regular customers and a friend. He was sitting with Vic, me, and the guys, and we all said, "You better check in." The public telephone was in the hallway by the men's room. I sneaked out to eavesdrop on Bob's conversation because he played the macho role. I overheard him say, "Yes, Dear, I'll stop by the store; yes, I will pick up little Bobby from practice. I'll have just *one more*. Yes, Honey Dumplin', I love you. I'll be home soon, bye bye, Darling." I ran back to my seat at the bar and told the guys. When he got back I asked, "Hey, Bobby, everything okay, what did you tell her?" Bob reared back in his seat and said, "I told that bitch to kiss my ass and I'll be home when I get there." We all cracked up.

One wild and crazy Friday evening, Big John was forced to break up a fight between a husband and wife. John physically threw the arrogant man out of the lounge. The flirtatious wife continued to party with her friends. A couple of hours later she left with a man through the side door. Approximately thirty minutes later, we heard an earth-shattering sound behind the lounge. I ran out and saw that the jealous husband had driven his automobile through the window of a motel room. He was trying to get out of his vehicle. Big John and I got to him. I told John to contain him and see if he was hurt. I pushed my way into the room. His wife and the man were in shock as they were struggling to get on their clothes. I made sure they weren't hurt while I called the police. The police arrived immediately and arrested the husband. Even though he created over two thousand dollars in damages, I felt sorry for the guy. He truly loved his wife while she treated him miserably. That wasn't the first time she had left with another man. Thank God, this time, no one was hurt.

Still trusting and naïve, I never realized that friends and customers used and sold drugs. Everyone knew how I felt about the evil of our society. Yes, I know I pushed booze for a living, but not the deadly kind. In later years, I would find out that two leading businesses were built on the selling of drugs—a florist company and a world famous surf shop.

Vic and I were clean in every aspect, even though the county vice squad was always spying on us. One officer, the redneck Mike Sullivan, in particular harassed the business. There may have been several reasons—personal (Vic did his girlfriend), sexy women always at the bar, the variety of characters as our clientele, or Artie, a black man in our group, dating a white woman. We didn't care or worry, until he tried to set us up. Late one Friday night, while Sullivan was spying on his girlfriend or running a surveillance on the place, a couple of men dragged him out of his unmarked car and beat him severely. A customer came in the lounge and said there was a fight in the parking lot. Vic and John jumped up and said they would handle the situation. A few minutes later they came in the lounge and told Frank, the bartender, to call an ambulance. The next morning Vic told me that he had a couple of friends from Miami "have a talk" with Mike. Then he asked me to call Steve Dewitt, a good friend and a captain with the sheriff's department, to tell him about Mike's harassing. From that day on, we never heard from Sullivan again. Vic and I disagreed on how he handled the situation.

On the brighter side, we had installed mirrors on the ceilings of two rooms and called them our Honeymoon Suites. We decorated them in red and glitter with heartshaped beds. Wow, were they tacky! Oddly enough, they sold out every weekend. While on duty one Saturday morning, I was talking to Mary Lou, our front-office manager, when a good old boy came to the desk. We both said, "Good morning, sir, how was everything?"

He was a honeymooner from Georgia in one of our special rooms. He said, "Great—got married to my sweetheart, got drunk and got laid last night. But this morn', where them-there mirrors are—it was tough shaving and I damn near drowned trying to brush my tooths!" We all laughed and got him a cup of coffee.

Vic and I were working hard and playing harder. We had some excess cash flow for investment. Vic talked me into becoming a partner in The Missile Lounge—a strip joint! This was an experience, to say the least. I thought there was no stopping me. With another partner, I bought another closed lounge. I drew up a business plan and named it The Hospital. I had bartenders dressed as doctors, and the cocktail waitresses as nurses. We installed flashing lights and bought an ambulance to drive home excessive drinkers. The Ladies Hospital Auxiliary called and complained about the theme. It took a while but the Hospital caught on, particularly Fridays and Saturdays.

I was burning the candle at both ends and the middle. Vic was concentrating on the Missile Lounge while I was between the other two locations. Vic was importing better strippers and acts. One afternoon while we were having a drink in the office, in walks Cha-Cha as beautiful as ever. I was in amazement as Vic laughed and said, "Surprise." He said that he had seen her in Miami and had to have her (in every way).

She said, "Okay, which one first? Let's get it out of the way."

I said, "That's not necessary. Let's stick to business."

Vic said, "Speak for yourself, Chance." I left and would come back to see her perform. She was a smashing hit with the old duffers as well as the young studs. Even the women liked her. That's when I thought, it's a small world and the past will find you out. She worked out fine, and when she left we were good friends.

The mid-Seventies brought a disaster to the hospitality industry. Locally the Space Center had constantly laid off until the area faced an alarming unemployment rate of 28 percent! Motel/hotel occupancies were at an all-time low. Nationally, gas prices had hit an all-time high: $1.50 a gallon! The traveling public was at an all-time low. Thanks to our wonderful federal government and OPEC, hospitality was suffering and going out of business. With the coming of Disney World, investors had overbuilt in the Orlando market. Throughout Florida, motel rooms were being sold for eight to twelve dollars per night!

I began to see the handwriting on the wall. The motel occupancy dropped from 68 percent to 35 percent. All the lounges began to decrease in revenue. Vic began to act different as did my other partner. Being young and trusting, I never believed anyone would steal from me. I now realized that I had overextended myself. I also realized that I was off course with my career. Vic and C.D. met with me and informed me that we should give the property back to the mortgage company. This we did, and I dissolved my other partnerships. Vic had signed his assets over to his father-in-law, and I got a notice from the Internal Revenue Service. I finally paid the judgment on a monthly payment plan. Jo-Jo forgave me and stood by me as usual. I quit drinking and pulled myself together. Working for yourself is not as great as everyone thinks. I decided that I needed to get back to the real hotel business. I began to mail out resumes.

The first five years of the Seventies started slow but finished fast—exciting and disappointing. We enjoyed great athletes such as Joe Frazier, George Foreman, Muhammad Ali, Mark Spitz, Secretariat, Hank Aaron, Jack Nicklaus, and the undefeated Miami Dolphins. The

Vietnam War ended as did the military draft. Watergate and the resignation of President Nixon shocked the world. It was the beginning of discos, bell-bottoms, encounter groups, women jockeys and generals, Mickey Mouse watches, and Disney World. The entertainment world gave us *Jesus Christ Superstar, The Wiz, All in the Family, The Godfather, Cabaret, Happy Days, Jaws,* Three Dog Night, Chicago, The Jacksons, The Osmonds, *2001: A Space Odyssey, Sanford and Son,* Rod Stewart, Creedence, David Bowie, and Alice Cooper. I wondered what the next five years would bring to us and the country.

CHAPTER 3

ORLANDO, ST. AUGUSTINE, JACKSONVILLE, WASHINGTON D.C., NORTH CAROLINA AND VIRGINIA

1975

After returning from an adventurous and relaxing trip to England, I had received several letters in reference to my resumé. While in England, I had the pleasure of meeting Jo-Jo's great family (I mean "clan'). I was pleasantly surprised when I heard from six hotel companies, and in turn I accepted four interviews. In one week I flew to Atlanta, Dallas, and Memphis. The next week I drove to Orlando and had an informative interview with Mr. Richard Bromley. He was president of the National Hospitality Management Corporation (NHMC). Mr. Bromley was very impressive when presenting his company. He and his partner were experienced hotel men who had formed a management company. As I mentioned before, Orlando had overbuilt. While OPEC and our own government were ripping off the general public, the traveling public limited their travel distance drastically. The financial institutions were foreclosing on hotels and motels throughout the country. Real Estate Investment Trusts (REITs) were in serious trouble because so many had invested in the hospitality industry. Mr. Bromley's partner, David Libberman, had an inside track with a couple of strong financial institutions—Chase Manhattan Bank and Charter

Mortgage Corporation. They began with two management contracts in Pennsylvania and contracted to manage two more hotels in Florida. They were searching for two young general managers.

Early in the following week, I received two interesting offers from the Holiday Inn Corporation and a Hilton franchisee. On Friday Mr. Bromley called me and offered me a GM's position in Orlando. I thought over the offers and talked to Jo-Jo about each one. I felt that I would have a better opportunity with a smaller company. We accepted Bromley's offer, and I would meet him Monday at the American Inn (a two-hundred-unit property) located on the ever-popular, overcrowded International Drive. International Drive was an overdeveloped strip of hotels, motels, franchised fast-food operations, and T-shirt shops located five miles from Walt Disney World. With the thought of getting a spinoff of the Disney traffic, developers and investors continued to build. Every other property on the Drive was either in Chapter 11 or operated by a financial institution. All the hotel franchise signs were there—Holiday Inn, Hilton Inn, Sheraton, Quality Inn, Days Inn, Travelodge, Best Western, Howard Johnson, and Rodeway Inn, as well as a couple of independents.

I arrived early on Monday morning at the property. I picked up a steaming cup of coffee next door at the 7-11 store and waited anxiously for Mr. Bromley's arrival. As I was studying the inn, the suits came through the lobby doors. The only person I recognized was Mr. Bromley. He looked straight at me and addressed me ever so politely and cheerfully—"Good morning, Mr. Wayne." He excused himself from the others and said that he needed to speak with me. He explained to me that we were taking over the property at 9:00 A.M. that morning! He said that we acquired the management contract from Charter Mortgage Corporation. Mr. Bromley introduced me to Mr. Howard, the former owner; Mr. Atkinson, the mortgage company representative; and Mr. Trump, an attorney. We all headed toward the innkeeper's office. Mr. Howard spoke to Jean Austin, the GM's secretary, and asked for the manager. She replied that he cleared out his desk and left yesterday. We looked at one another, and Mr. Howard with a heavy Southern accent said, "Let's get on with it!!"

We went across the hall to a meeting room. The attorney began by laying out the basis of the agreement between the three parties. Mr. Howard was a gentleman from Alabama who had made his fortune in the dairy business. He then built two hotels in the Orlando area and let his relatives manage the properties. Today he was going to lose both of them. As Mr. Trump read each party's responsibilities, Mr. Howard's eyes began to cloud up. I was not expecting this sad chain of events. This was known as a "friendly takeover." Mr. Howard walked away clean and took his losses. The mortgage company took back the property and hired a professional management company. The takeover time was also the cut-off time. At 9:00 A.M. that day, all past accounts payable, payroll taxes, and accounts receivable would belong to Mr. Howard. This was all new to me. Even though I just started a new job, a very nice man just lost two hotels—the American Inn and the Howard Johnson Hotel. I thought to myself, what a sad avenue to acquire a position. Mr. Howard was a gentleman throughout the changeover. With Jean's assistance we verified house banks, receivables, and payables, and we punched the employees out and immediately punched them back in on the time clocks. Jean called the department heads and asked them to bring all their keys to the office. We reviewed and verified all the keys of the hotel. Mr. Howard turned them over to Mr. Bromley, and he in turn passed them to me. We called a general staff meeting. Mr. Howard declined to stay, wished us good fortune, and immediately left the property. I was still rather choked up, but I had to show strength and confidence.

Mr. Bromley was a big, strapping, jolly gentleman with a broad smile for everyone. Dressed in a Hart, Schaffner and Marx pinstriped suit, he projected class with his powerful voice and precise vocabulary. As he began to speak to the staff, everyone in the room began to feel more relaxed and comfortable. He introduced himself, me, and the company. In simple terms he explained what event had just happened and reassured everyone that they would continue their employment if they so chose. He then smiled, looked Jean in the eye, and said, "Jean, tell Mr. Wayne and all of us about yourself." Jean was an overweight, outgoing, well-dressed lady in her late thirties. As Jean finished telling everyone about herself, the staff loosened up and everyone introduced themselves and told us a little something about themselves.

Mr. Bromley continued by revealing his plans for the hotel, and one could then feel the excitement in the room. He was quite a motivational speaker. He then looked straight into my eyes and said, "Mr. Wayne, meet your team, and I know you will lead them successfully!" Wow, Mr. Bromley was a hard act to follow, as I knew he was testing me. I cleared my throat, looked around the conference room, put on my best Sunday smile, and slowly looked into the face of everyone as I gazed around the room. I then said, "That was our head coach and I will be your quarterback and hope to always lead in a winning way. I will meet with each of you in each department." Everyone appeared to be settled as Mr. Bromley thanked them for their time and sent them back to their jobs. Mr. Bromley asked if I would be all right since he had to go downtown to the Howard Johnson Hotel. I assured him everything would be done by company policy and agreement. He asked me to be available if he needed me downtown. He excused himself in his charming manner.

Jean and I dug in for the task ahead. A few hours later Mr. Bromley called and asked about things. He continued by asking if I would meet him tomorrow to inventory the Ho Jo property. Jean ordered in food, and we continued working until the night auditor arrived. I met with John, the auditor, to explain what had occurred and what we needed to do in order to close out. At first John was a little cold and strange but as we worked through the night, he felt more comfortable. I sent Jean home at midnight and I retired at about 3:00 A.M. I had called Jo-Jo earlier to advise her that I would be staying over.

Still full of excitement and running on pure adrenaline, I met Mr. Bromley at the Howard Johnson Hotel. He introduced me to the staff and we got to work immediately. We finished early in the afternoon as the corporate controller arrived. Mr. Bromley asked me to assist him if needed. After a couple hours I felt that I should go back to the American Inn. When I arrived, everything was well. The staff and I adjusted to one another quickly.

I reviewed the property in detail in order that I could prepare a capital budget, an operating budget, and a marketing plan. Mr. Bromley was big on budgets and plans. Later I found out why—as he put it, we had to be prepared for the "dog and pony show." More numbers, forecasts, and written plans with goals impressed the bankers. I had written a simple plan before, but when Mr. Bromley got through with me, I could write a sophisticated book that included every way to sell a room to every person in every walk of life. But he knew that I knew this was strictly a tourist and bus property. That was the market on which we were to concentrate our efforts. As I drove the parking lots of our competitors, I would make note of the bus companies in their parking lots.

One evening as I was leaving the property, I spotted Harris Rosen; he was the executive assistant manager at the Cape Kennedy Hilton when I was hired there. He was doing the same thing that I was. I shouted "Harris." He stopped and we chatted. He was also a very clever fellow, and I knew that he would do well. He had put together a deal and bought the Quality Inn on International Drive. Harris was very aggressive in the bus business. If I had a bus group at twelve dollars a room, he would offer a ten-dollar rate. Eventually, Harris became the bus "king," and his hotel was full while the other properties struggled. Then there was Cecil Day with his Days Inns selling rooms for eight dollars a night. Average room rates were disgraceful! Even without a major flag (franchise), we held our own through several outlets and networking schemes.

Not only did we concentrate on the bus business, we were very aggressive in the senior market (which most hotels overlooked). International Drive Hotels and Motels were in a price war. What a crazy world—gas was at $1.50 a gallon, but you could buy a 20¢ hamburger and a $8.00 room. With OPEC controlling the price of oil, bus and airline travel was flat with no increase. Automotive travel had decreased drastically. The public traveled closer to home for shorter vacations.

With no debt service and good management in place, the Inn began to turn around financially. The mortgage company seemed happy, the company was receiving their fees, and I now had a good solid staff. Jo-Jo and I were happy again as I was only forty-five minutes from our beach home. Late one evening, Mr. Bromley called me at home and informed me the company was taking over another property in St. Augustine, Florida. This was the beginning of the end of our easy, comfortable life. After six months, I had earned Mr. Bromley's respect and confidence. He instructed me to meet him at midnight in three days at the new property.

When I arrived at "my" property on Monday morning, everything was good until the afternoon. While walking the property, I noticed a small child splashing at the end of the pool. People were sunbathing, sipping drinks, talking, and listening to loud radios. I could see the child was in trouble. Without thinking, I dived into the swimming pool, grabbed the child, and tossed her out on the ledge of the pool. I began practicing CPR on the blue-skinned, brown-eyed little beauty. She began coughing and out came the water. Her little face became white with fear as she began crying in relief. Her mother finally ran over screaming and began reaching for the little girl. I was extremely happy and thankful for the child, but I was very angry with her parents. I asked her, "Where the hell were you? That beautiful little girl almost died because of your neglect!"

She began, "I just went to the room for a minute and I thought her Daddy was out here." I went and called the paramedics to ensure the safety of the child. I then went back to the pool and reminded everyone to read the posted pool rules. The little lady was only three years old. I wrote an incident report and sent copies to the corporate office. As I said earlier, the hotel business can be different every day—especially dealing with the crazy public.

I appointed Jean as MOD and left to meet Mr. Bromley at the Family Inns of America. It was a cute little one-hundred-unit highway budget property. This time it was just Mr. Bromley and myself for this takeover contract. We went through the same procedural exercise. We finished before sunrise, got another cup of coffee and waited for the staff to arrive. Again, we found out that the innkeeper had left before we arrived. Mr. Bromley called for another staff meeting and gave his Dale Carnegie speech. We met everyone, went over company policy, and sent them to their respective jobs. Mr. Bromley then turned to me and said, "Chance, since this is only a hundred-room property with no food and beverage, could you put together the budget and marketing plan by next week?"

I answered, "Certainly!"

He smiled and continued, "Also, keep an eye on both properties until I get a manager for this inn." He grabbed his well-worn bag and headed toward Jacksonville to meet his partner at the bank. For a mover and shaker in the hotel industry, not only did he have the knowledge, he had manners and class.

Jo-Jo drove up to meet and work with me on the weekend. We inspected the property thoroughly and were very unhappy because of the lack of cleanliness and poor maintenance. Jo made the notes and I met with Doris, the executive housekeeper, and Daren, the maintenance chief. The housekeeper immediately became defensive as I was pointing out certain items. The chief began with explanations—no money to do the proper job. I said, "With no supplies, tools, and other items needed this is understandable—but dirt is dirt!" At that point, the big-mouth, negative woman jumped out of her chair and said, "I don't need this. I can stay home and make more money from welfare, food stamps, and unemployment." She stomped out as Daren and I looked at one another. Now Daren started telling me about all the staff (some things I didn't want to know). I told him to make a wish list, thanked him, and sent him back to work. I had to call Jo-Jo and tell her what Doris had said. That's a heck of a note when our government supports lazy people! Over the years, I observed that the laziest employees are always the ones that complain the most!

I promoted the assistant housekeeper, hired a couple of people, ordered everything the property needed, gave each department a list of items that needed to be done, set up a new bank account, and began working on the budgets and marketing plan. With working late hours, I finished everything by Tuesday morning. Since it was fall and business was slow, I felt I could go back to Orlando until next Friday. Jo-Jo went back to Cocoa Beach and I went back to the American Inn.

When I arrived at the Inn, I met with Jean. She informed me that we lost two housekeepers and one room clerk—otherwise all else was fine. But we needed to keep our eye on Harry, the bartender. Jean knows he is hitting on all the females and possibly trying to push prostitutes. I confronted him when he arrived for his shift. With his jive talk, he tried to talk to me as one of his buddies and said that he would cut me into the action. I interrupted and dismissed him on the spot. As I was bartending for the evening, my mind regressed to twelve years ago to Tampa. Times change, people change, situations change, and companies have different philosophies. That is just the reason I did not become a minister—if you can't live it, don't preach it! This had been a long day—5:00 A.M. in St. Augustine to 1:00 A.M. in Orlando. My "dogs" were killing me.

The next morning, I called Mr. Bromley and brought him up to date on both properties. He in turn gave me some more sales leads and informed me that we should be taking over more properties in the near future. At the time, all types of creative financing were being developed. As we all have hindsight, I realize now I should have created a deal to buy the American Inn. Business there continued to increase as did Ho Jo's. Even the little Roadside Inn in St. Augustine began to show some progress. Even though I began to average seventy hours-plus per week, we all enjoyed personal satisfaction. As a small management company, we continued to grow. Mr. Bromley and Mr.

Libberman had reached eight contracts with several pending. I felt that I had made the right decision.

One evening about 11:00 P.M. I received a call from my flaky night auditor at the American Inn. He proceeded to go into one of his long excuses for not being able to work that night. I stopped him and said, "Don't bother, I can do your job!" This young man did this quite frequently, especially on weekends. I got my second wind, called the second-shift clerk, and told her that I was on my way. As the night progressed, all was going well and grew very quiet. This reminded me of the Tahitian when I would rush to get my work complete in order that I would have time to do my school homework. I had to drink a pot of coffee to stay awake until two young black men rushed into the lobby. The first young man asked, "How much is a room?" I began to say "$19.95," when the second young man pulled a gun and said, "Then we will take all of them!" He was nervous as he waved the pistol in my face. The other man jumped across the front desk and pulled out the cash drawer. He asked, "Is this all?"

I said, "Please don't shoot. Take it all. I only work here part-time. Man, I got a family!"

The man behind the desk pushed me, jumped over the desk, and they both ran out. I breathed a sigh of relief and felt very lucky. I immediately called the police. They arrived in a few minutes. They questioned me and I gave them a description of both men as well as the tag number of the getaway car. They only stole $150. The next day, a detective called me to come down and make an identification. These silly young men, in their early twenties, were caught in a couple of hours. I made the ID, and they were off to hard time. As I thanked God, I thought, what a shame. After being up for two and a half days, I slept for twelve hours. Jo-Jo would not let anyone disturb me.

One bright and sunny morning, Mr. Bromley called me and told me to prepare for another "dog and pony" show. He informed me that the bankers and a prospective buyer will be at the property in the afternoon. After I hung up, I thought: What have I done, worked myself out of a job? The standard operating procedure (SOP) is that the first person to be gone is the innkeeper! After the inspection of the property, the banker winked at me and said, "Chance, the property looks great as well as the increase in occupancy." Mr. Admir, the potential purchaser, thanked me and they left. I promptly called Mr. Bromley and passed along what had occurred. In return, he assured me that I would continue employment with him. He continued by advising me of three more management contracts to close within thirty days.

As the area continued to recover, Disney World was becoming a world vacation destination and, as with any other tourist mecca, here came the riffraff. Not only did International Drive suffer from room thefts, car thefts, and even a couple of muggings, so did Lake Buena Vista and properties near Disney.

The newly formed Central Florida Hotel/Motel Association became involved with the sheriffs' departments. Being somewhat outspoken with my big mouth, I was elected to the Board. We set up certain rooms in selected properties with undercover tourists. Within two weeks the undercover cops busted two thieves on

International Drive and two on the U.S. Highway 192 strip. After the investigation, we were informed that a family from the north was behind the theft ring. One member was a maintenance man at three different properties in the area within the past eighteen months. When Jake Henry was arrested, three copies of master keys from the three hotels were found in his possession. The law enforcement agencies asked us to run a better past employment check. We, in turn, asked if they could create an ID card for hospitality employees. They told the association that they would get back with us.

Meanwhile, Mr. Bromley called and said that we needed to meet tomorrow evening. As usual, Mr. Bromley was gracious as he invited me and Jo-Jo to dinner. He informed us that the mortgage companies had sold both the St. Augustine Inn and the American Inn. While Jo-Jo and I probably looked stunned, he flashed his big broad smile and said, "Chance, I have you an even bigger challenge in Jacksonville Beach." He asked me to wrap up both properties with the individual new owners. He also informed me that they wanted to hire me to continue operating the Inns. He jokingly said, "I got a deal you can't refuse." He seriously thanked me, asked me to stay with him, and handed me an envelope. We enjoyed a lovely dinner and left. When Jo-Jo and I got home, I opened the envelope—a thousand-dollar check as a bonus. What a classy guy!

Meanwhile, I had become involved in the community per our marketing plan. I had to resign from the Chamber of Commerce and The Hotel/Motel Association. As we did when I joined the company, I made the changeover of both properties within one week. Jo-Jo and I took a vacation to Las Vegas before we began our new opportunity in Jax Beach, Florida.

At the time of the sales, I didn't realize that this was the beginning of the movement for major investments by Middle Eastern individuals and groups within the hotel industry. As in later years, this group would influence the business greatly since they run their businesses differently than other operators.

Jo-Jo and I apparently could not have children, so we began the adoption process. We met with adoption agencies and attorneys to review many cases of young children. One of Jo-Jo's customers mentioned a special case in which a beautiful little boy needed a good home. We pursued this special situation and adopted a sick little boy named Mark William Walker. This was a thrill for the both of us—instant parents. Mark was quiet and could not speak. Jo-Jo planned to sell her shop to concentrate on raising and nursing Mark back to health. She did this within weeks. We sold the beauty salon and commercial building as Jo-Jo and Mark joined me in Jacksonville Beach.

I had arrived earlier at Jax Beach to face a rundown oceanfront Quality Inn Hotel. I had met Mr. Bromley, the bank representatives, and the arrogant general manager. He didn't want to give up the property or the records. He did when the court order was presented. At that point the transaction became a hostile takeover. The GM stomped out of the meeting and took a couple of the staff members with him. Since each property has its own personality, I had to find it myself with no help. We did our marketing plan, operating budget, and a very exciting capital budget:

one million dollars! We planned a total renovation of the hotel, new restaurant and lounge, and the addition of meeting facilities to accommodate up to five hundred persons.

After replacing some key staff members, the new team began functioning and operating the hotel efficiently. Even with "excuse our dust, expansion is a must" signs throughout the property, we struggled through the next few months. During this time, Jo-Jo served as our public relations person as well as our lifeguard. We lived in the hotel, which gave Jo-Jo the time to be a mother to Mark and to assist me in my work. Within those months, we became a solid, happy family.

Even during construction, we surpassed our budgeted revenues. Our designers did a beautiful, exciting job and were ahead of schedule. Mr. Bromley, the sales department, and I were planning the elegant grand opening of the oceanfront Golden Pelican restaurant, Bogie's Bar, and the Oceans convention center. The designers completed an outstanding decor in appointing the rooms and suites in tropical light and airy colors. All two hundred units were oceanfront with balconies. The lobby and public areas featured live tropical plants, marble floors, and restful tropical colors. The atmosphere and excitement in the air began to build as the magical date drew near. The marketing plan was in effect, the sales blitz complete, the invitations mailed, advertisements in place, and the new sign was being installed—The Sheraton Beach Resort.

Mr. Bromley helped me staff the property with an award-winning French chef, André, and an Italian food and beverage director, Luigi. I was very fortunate to complete the balance of my staff with professionals—Helga, a German executive housekeeper; a beautiful Southern sales manager, Jessica; a blonde English front-office manager, David; and a black chief engineer, Tyrone. What a wonderful, balanced, international staff lead by a Florida "cracker"! Between all my staff they could speak six languages. Mr. Bromley knew how to impress the local bankers. He helped plan and lay out the grand opening. We had invited all the media, corporate heads, community leaders, politicians, local celebrities, military and government leaders, local business owners, educational and professional community, as well as the governor and his staff.

For three days, the restaurant staff practiced serving the rest of the hotel staff and their families. I had written a schedule for all employees to be treated as guests. We worked hard to prepare and have fun at the same time. When the big day arrived, we were ready for the gigantic VIP party. Everyone stood tall in their uniforms wearing a big smile. The department heads, Jo-Jo, and myself were formally dressed as we greeted our guests at the front doors of the lobby. Other staff members escorted our guests to the exotically decorated convention center. André, Luigi, and the food and beverage staff did an elaborate job of the food presentation—colored ice carvings, fountains, designs of platters, flambé stations, exotic drink bars, floral arrangements, and upbeat island music by the most popular local band. It didn't take long before certain public areas were overcrowded. We invited over eight hundred people and it appeared they all showed up with friends. All went well except the kitchen got in the weeds with the food, and at times we needed five more bars. At the end of the day, all went well, everyone went home full and happy. Most of all, we received an excellent review from the media, the bankers were pleased, and my bosses very satisfied because we opened at an 80 percent occupancy. It was a party similar to the Hilton's opening. It appeared to be a smashing success, since the next night (Friday) there was an hour wait at the restaurant, two deep at the bar while the convention center was accommodating a three-hundred-person banquet. We all put in average twelve-hour days for the past week, but it was worth the effort. I took off Sunday with the family to enjoy the beach.

Back to work Monday, all the staff reported to work and we were off and running. Through the week we drew a high market share of the corporate and government accounts and filled weekends with the leisure travelers. At this time every type of discount was being born: the corporate rate, the AAA rate, the senior rate, the government rate, the military rate, the travel agent rate, the airline discount, bus tour rate, the wholesale rate, the net rate, the long-stay rate, the weekend rate, the package rate, and any promotional rate deemed necessary. What ever happened to the rack (published) rate, which was the average room rate (ADR) used to prepare the budgets?

The sales department and I continued to make sales calls. We landed several interesting accounts such as the U.S. Marshall's office, the local dinner theatre, and the navy account at Mayport Naval Station. Also we were the first good hotel near Ponte Vedra, home of the Tournament Players Championship (TPC). Of course, we had two strong weeks during the football season. The great southern rivalry between the Florida Gators and the Georgia Bulldogs (the world's largest outdoor cocktail party) filled the cities. We always anxiously awaited the announcement of the two teams that would meet in the annual Gator Bowl contest. Not only did we seek to house the teams, we concentrated on the alumni. The alumni were even better because we didn't have to discount the rooms, and our food and beverage sales skyrocketed!

The TPC week was another exciting week with the golf pros and the media choosing our hotel. Our friends, Tony Lord (former cruiserweight British boxer), his wife, Jo-Jo, and I had the pleasure of seeing and meeting Lee Trevino, Jack Nicklaus, and Gary Player. That was the first time they were ever paired together. Lee was loose and talking to the gallery while Jack and Gary were their serious selves. Lee won the richest tournament up to that time on the tour.

As said many times, "timing is everything." Being the general manager of a first-class, popular hotel brought many perks to me and my family. We were invited to all community functions and special events. We attended the captain's VIP party on the British HMS *Hermes* Aircraft Carrier. As Jo-Jo and I had too much wine, we bid goodnight. Jo-Jo bid farewell in her royal fashion and her expensive gold bracelet flowed off her wrist into the Atlantic Ocean! Another treasure at the bottom of the Atlantic. The British Navy gave the hotel a great deal of business with no problems, but for some of the U.S. Navy members, that was another story.

The Alpha Dinner Theatre proved to be an extremely valuable account. We contracted a fifty-two-week agreement to provide accommodations for all their casts.

My family and I had the pleasure of meeting several stars such as Ann Margaret, Jack Kelly, James Drury, and Forrest Tucker. They were a sheer delight to have as guests! Mr. Forrest Tucker invited Jo-Jo's mother, Jo-Jo, Mark, and myself to join him on several occasions for lunch or dinner. As a big, rough, and rugged character, Mr. Tucker was kind, gentle, and funny. At the dining table he was having fun with our little Mark. Mark recognized him from the *F Troop* TV series. He told Mark to punch him in the jaw. Mark smiled, balled up his little fist, and gave him a "sock." Mr. Tucker shocked the whole table and dining room and spit out his bridge! Mark's eyes were big as light bulbs and said that he was sorry. Mr. Tucker reared back with a huge, deep, hearty laugh. He pulled his bridge back in and stood up. He was a giant of a man. He kissed the ladies' hands, gave me and Mark a firm handshake, grabbed the check, thanked us, and excused himself. He was running a little late to the theatre. What a gentleman! Before he left the hotel (after six weeks), he invited my family and me to visit him at his ranch in Arizona.

Even after the newness wore off, a year later the hotel was enjoying a good occupancy and the Golden Pelican still had waiting lists. Bogie's was still the in spot, and the banquet department was constantly busy. Again, we were enjoying the good life. That didn't last long. Mr. Bromley called and asked me to meet him in Asheville, North Carolina, at the Landmark Hotel. With the fine staff I had, I was comfortable to leave the property.

When I arrived at our designated meeting spot, Mr. Bromley wasn't there. I didn't know what to think since the hotel was closed. I spoke with the security guard and he told me that this sleek, new hotel had closed four weeks ago. Mr. Bromley arrived, and we were shown throughout the property. We left and checked into the Asheville Hilton. We met for dinner and he shared his thoughts. He and his partner had met with the mortgage holder. Mr. Bromley told me in order to acquire the management contract, they had to sign a letter of intent to purchase. We spent a week in the city and completed a feasibility study. Mr. Bromley thanked me and headed home. I was anxious to return to Jax Beach.

After arriving home, all was well, until the third week. The contract with the U.S. Marshall's office was working great. My department heads and I knew the arrangement. The federal witnesses were always in an eighth floor room, just down the hall from our apartment. On this fatal weekend, three young people checked in late Saturday night. They insisted on a ground-floor room in order to walk directly to the beach. On Monday morning, Ms. Emma, our oldest housekeeper, came to my office and told me that the D.N.D. (Do Not Disturb) sign had been on for two days. I called Room 114 and there was no answer. We went to the room and knocked very loudly and said, "Housekeeping." We repeated our actions. There was no answer, so I opened the door with my master key. As we entered the very dark room, there was a very strange, sickly odor. As I turned on the lights, the room was a mess and in disarray with someone laying across the bed. As I approached the body, Ms. Emma screamed and passed out. She had turned on the bathroom lights and spotted a bloody, half-nude body in the bathtub. I put a cold cloth on Ms. Emma's forehead. I helped her out of the room as Ms.

Helga arrived. She helped her to my office. Upon further investigation, I found another body partially under the second bed. It appeared that all three young people had been stabbed to death directly in the heart. I secured the room and immediately called the police. They responded rapidly and took charge. They immediately questioned me, Ms. Emma, and the rest of my staff. I called Mr. Bromley to advise him of the tragedy. He asked me to keep it as quiet as possible. I did, but not Deputy Dog. Detective Murphy took charge and was spouting off to the press until the Feds arrived. They took over the case and shut everyone out. Yes, you guessed it: two witnesses and an innocent bystander. The two young men and beautiful young girl were from Virginia Beach, Virginia, and were key witnesses in a major drug case. It appeared the Feds made a mistake while a contract was fulfilled. As of today, the case has not been solved. Strangely, there were no complaints of noise from the adjoining rooms, which were occupied. By policy, I sent an incident report to the corporate office. Of course, our liability insurance carrier contacted me. I felt uneasy as did Ms. Emma for quite a time. I gave Ms. Emma a one-week paid vacation. The family and I went to Orlando to visit my parents.

When I returned to the hotel, I had a message to call Mr. Bromley. This time he asked me to go to Wilmington, North Carolina, and "baby-sit" the Riverside Hilton Hotel. When I arrived, the staff greeted me cordially upon check-in. I immediately called a staff meeting and informed everyone to continue as usual. I was overseeing the operation until the new innkeeper would arrive.

The next night, Friday, proved interesting. As I walked the property, I noticed a poster by the ballroom. It featured the talented Ink Spots for that night only. I saw ladies and gentlemen arriving in their gowns and tuxedos carrying brown bags. I called Eric, the food and beverage director, and asked him about the liquor in the brown bags, which looked strange. Several bars were set up but with only soft drinks, mixers, and ice.

Eric laughed, and with his New York accent said, "Mr. Wayne, you will not believe these hypocritical liquor laws in this state. At this point in time, we cannot sell liquor by the drink, but they can bring their own bottle." He laughed again and said, "It gets worse. They need to drink the entire bottle because the other law is that you can't have an open container of alcohol in your vehicle." We got a soda and continued laughing about the old blue laws that exist throughout the country. In a few counties, the law only allows the sale of miniatures. In Tennessee where Jack Daniels is distilled, the county was dry. In some counties, you can buy beer and wine on Sunday but not liquor. Some states at the time had eighteen-year-old laws, but most did not. If a "kid" can serve (maybe die for) his/her country, why can't he/she have a drink? In some counties, one cannot buy a drink in a cocktail lounge but can have a cocktail in a private club. There are still some powerful moonshiners even today. Oh well, in time these and other strange laws will be changed and we'll arrive in the twenty-first century.

I installed the corporate paper flow and coasted until the new GM arrived. Jim Swank, an experienced hotel man, relieved me. I returned to Jax Beach.

When I got back to the hotel, all was fine except in the food department. The kitchen was filthy and the grand ballroom was dirty. The restaurant could have looked better. Luigi took my criticism well, but André took it very personally. Plus he wore filthy uniforms and did not use deodorant. Maybe I came down too hard on him, which embarrassed him. André didn't speak to me for a couple of days. I understood temperamental executive chefs!

Jo-Jo and I usually ate in the Pelican every Friday evening and tried the chef's special. That particular evening the special was Florentine Rainbow Trout. It tasted good at the time, but in the middle of the night we both woke up extremely ill. We were so sick that we could not go to the hospital. I called the front desk and they reached the hotel doctor. Dr. Watkins came over promptly and diagnosed that we had been poisoned by something we had eaten or drank! He gave us a prescription to clear our systems. Was this coincidental or intentional? We completely recovered in forty-eight hours, and today we feel this was intentional. I never could prove it, but I did arrange for André to be transferred. After this incident, I became paranoid and spent more time in the kitchen.

As time went on, I began to notice more new suits snooping around the hotel. I called Mr. Bromley and asked, "What's happening?" He always shot straight with me and said he didn't know but would be down to see me.

He arrived the next evening. We met the following morning for breakfast and he said, "Chance, I think you worked yourself out of a job again." With a big smile, he said, "We have just acquired two more contracts, and I think the bank is now actively trying to sell this property.

After two years, you have done a great job, business is up and that's time to sell. Mortgage holders do not want to be in the hotel business. It is only real estate to them. They have no idea about the hospitality business." He reassured me about my future and asked me to continue to be positive and not to share this conversation with the staff. I didn't know how to tell Jo-Jo but she was a real trouper. She always stood by me in my career.

A couple of months passed, and Mr. Bromley finally called and informed me that the hotel had been sold. He said, "Write yourself a twenty-five-hundred-dollar bonus check, plan your vacation for thirty days, and afterwards meet me and David in Washington, D.C."

This was a very sad day for me, my family, our friends, and the staff. We had a good life, active in the community and church. Above all, we were happy and content with our lives. This crazy hotel business does not allow for a normal life. I made another smooth transition to the new owners, packed the family in our van and headed on holiday. We toured South Florida—Miami Beach, Ft. Lauderdale, the Seminole Indian Reservation—enjoyed an exciting airboat ride, and marveled at the sunset in Key West. We then returned home to Cocoa Beach to prepare for our trip to D.C.

I drove up the beautiful eastern seaboard in September, which was pleasant and colorful. I had a scheduled meeting with Stanley Kahn, Bromley, and Libberman at One Jefferson Circle Apartments near Georgetown. Upon arriving at the property, the manager met me and showed me to a nice, average two-bedroom apartment overlooking the gardens. I thought—what am I doing here? This would be a great suite hotel. Is this why I am here? I had become Mr. Bromley's troubleshooter, and I did enjoy the challenges.

I met the gentlemen the next morning in the small, dark, traditional lobby. Kahn began immediately, telling the partners what he wanted and expected. He revealed the blueprints and plans. The plans were to convert this apartment house into a suite hotel. This young, aggressive gentleman appeared to be very progressive and could see the new trend in the hospitality industry. Six blocks from the property was the Guest Quarters, the first suite hotel chain.

Stanley looked me directly in the eyes and said, "Chance, the guys tell me you are the hotel man. I expect you to help me make the conversion to a hotel successful and make me a lot of money." We reviewed and discussed the plans until 8:00 P.M., at which time we broke for dinner. We dined downstairs at the delightful French restaurant, Chez Louie's. After dinner, the ever-classy Mr. Bromley picked up the check. Stanley left, and we continued working late into the night.

The next morning I met Mr. Bromley, Libberman, Stanley's girlfriend Alexis, and the designer, Maurice. The plan was that Alexis would supervise the design and refurbishing of the property while I set up operations and marketing. She did ask me to lay out the front desk, which I did. Mr. Bromley and Libberman left to attend other meetings.

As I began to develop the business and marketing plans, I discovered that Washington, D.C., was very class-conscious and a phony metropolis. In this city, the businessmen wore a suit and tie every day. This Southerner began to adjust because the property had a choice location, at the beginning of Georgetown, on the Front Street of Embassy Row and only twelve blocks from the White House.

For the first few weeks, all was going well. I was interviewing for staff positions, writing and implementing policies and procedures, and setting up the departments. I got lucky upon hiring a secretary/administrative assistant. Harriet was a tall, attractive, lanky young lady who had related hotel experience and was savvy about the diabolical city. She was ambitious and dedicated to her job and me. We would work late on many occasions and have a late dinner and drinks on several evenings. On the second night of dining with Harriet, she became very familiar. As we finished our nightcaps, I felt Harriet's hand on my thigh and she whispered in my ear, "Mr. Wayne, would you take me home?" She continued to massage my thigh as well as my privates. She then licked her lips and said, "Boss, this is part of my obligation to you—which I want to do. This is expected of secretaries in Washington." Being a Southern gentleman, I agreed but informed Harriet that this was not part of her job description. When we arrived at her apartment, she took me by the hand with a strong grip and led me inside. When I left the next morning, I searched my soul again and questioned myself—why? This appeared to be the trend in business—boss-and-secretary affairs. This casual affair continued for a few weeks. I had to break it off because Jo-Jo was due in a few weeks. Harriet was very mature and accepted my decision as a cosmopolitan woman.

The designer and Alexis were always arguing in front of everyone. I also had the responsibility of evacuating the tenants, another very sad experience. Each day became more and more difficult dealing with the owner and his girlfriend. They were constantly in operations and upsetting the small staff that I had hired, which included an experienced administrative assistant, the sales manager from the Guest Quarters Hotel and his secretary, as well as an experienced Marriott executive housekeeper. Every time Alexis and I would have a problem, she would call Stanley; in turn Stanley would call Libberman, and David would call me. What a bunch of bull.

Meanwhile, Jo-Jo and Mark joined me, which helped me to maintain my sanity. I began to take off regular weekends to enjoy the family and the area. Jo-Jo advised me to be patient and learn to keep my mouth shut. This was difficult when designers create a beautiful work of art yet which is not functional in operating a successful hotel.

During this time, before the official opening, Mr. Bromley called me to meet him in Bryce Mountain, Virginia. He asked if I could get away for two weeks. I made arrangements and called him to advise him that we would be there in two days. The family and I had no idea where we were going until we bought a detailed map of the state. It appeared that our destination was only about three hours from D.C., a spectacular drive through the winding Virginia mountains. While dodging the deer, we came upon a magnificent sight. As we drove down the mountain, there appeared a quaint, charming community, the development known as Bryce Mountain. As we approached the township, we saw golf courses, townhouses, condos, an airstrip, a lodge, riding stables, stores, and ski slopes. We went to the lodge, and a beautiful townhouse was reserved in our name. I still didn't know why I was there, but we enjoyed our stay. I met Mr. Bromley for dinner, and he said that he needed me to work on the business plan for the revenue centers. This development was built as a getaway for the elite of the nation's capital (Joint Chiefs of Staff, senators, generals, etc.). The lodge housed a wonderful restaurant, a cocktail lounge, meeting facilities, and the ski operations. Jo-Jo and I were amazed to find out about snowmaking machines. What a magnificent view from the gorgeous, rustic lodge. I was excited to get started.

The operating director introduced me to the ski pro, golf pro, stable manager, lodge manager, and the comptroller. Our company was hired as a consulting firm. This was a wonderful break from the Washington project, and I began immediately. With the help of everyone, I had a great start on the plan. I decided to drag it out in order that the family and I could enjoy the facilities. With the beginning of the snow season, there was no snow! We saw the snow machines actually make snow and made our first attempt to ski. Jo-Jo and Mark did very well while I fell down the mountain. I commuted between properties for a month. I thought it was time that I should present my plan to Mr. Bromley. He thanked me, and the family headed back to D.C.

When I returned to the suites property, the staff was upset again. I had to re-create a good, work-friendly environment. We were getting close to the official opening even though with the "tight" ownership, we never actually closed the property as the date drew near. We began a very aggressive sales blitz. With everyone in Washington being so wrapped up in their own importance, seeing the person in charge was difficult. We soon found out that the secretaries were the most important people in D.C. We organized a "secretaries club," which was an instant success. They began to make reservations immediately to build their reward points.

As I previously mentioned, Embassy Row was behind the new suite hotel. As one may suspect, this street had several foreign embassies. They used the hotel frequently since we had good security and location.

Since we operated during renovation, we didn't have a true grand opening. We did advertise and received very good media coverage through our public relations program. Managing the property was most difficult because of pressure from Libberman, Alexis, and Stanley. I found out early in my career what micromanagement meant. Mr. Bromley spent most of his time with the other properties. If we did 79 percent occupancy, the question was why didn't you hit 80 percent occupancy? Even though business was good and improving, friction remained in the atmosphere because of the arrogant and demanding ownership. Even though my family and I enjoyed Washington, we were homesick for Florida and I wasn't happy with my situation.

Dealing with our foreign guests enlightened us to new cultures and thinking. They required special requests, foods, and demands. Prince Adikob from a Middle Eastern country used the hotel while in the United States as well as the Platinum Escort Service. Late one evening the front desk received several complaint calls about the presidential suite. Security investigated and was told to leave. Jason, the security officer, called me and I met him at the noisy suite. Loud music and screams had been coming from inside. I opened the suite with my master key and the prince began screaming, "How dare you, do you know who I am? I will sue you!" The bloody, beautiful blonde pulled free from the bully. We went downstairs to call the police as well as an ambulance. The girl was badly hurt. The police arrived. We filed a report and the girl said that she would file charges. When the officers found out who had committed the crime, they informed us that he had diplomatic immunity. I asked the officers to follow me and showed them how he destroyed the room. I asked the prince to leave and never come back to the hotel. He was highly insulted, but the officers escorted him off the property. What kind of laws are written in this country that allow foreigners into our great country to commit crimes and come and go as they please?

Speaking of our government, as a native citizen of this great country I have some observations. I had the opportunity to work with different government agencies on the local, state, and national levels. Most governmental departments appeared to work at 50 percent efficiency. If private businesses (which pay all the bills) did this, the entire nation would be in bankruptcy. The elected officials and bureaucrats should work toward a profit or at least a break-even point! But instead, they would always ask for an increase of their budgets rather than a decrease. An example of waste: Lockheed Corporation had an overrun of one-half billion dollars on just one project, but it still received a fifty-million-dollar bonus! Should the people hire specialized management companies to operate our own government?

While at the Jefferson Circle Hotel, I saw visitors from communist countries meeting with our elected officials, lobbyists, and corporate leaders. If only the walls of the hotel suites could talk. At one time, the CIA reviewed the registration of a certain week. A week later, the FBI confiscated the same records. A few months after I left the hotel, a Senate investigation was launched concerning the individuals that had secret meetings at the hotel. The city was beautiful, but the people who ran it and the country weren't! I knew that I had to leave and get away from this hypocritical, double-standard, and dangerous city. I called Mr. Bromley with no answer, so I drove to Maryland to see Libberman. I felt uncomfortable with these Ivy League, unethical scoundrels. I gave Libberman my notice and went back to the hotel to tell Jo-Jo and Mark. Within a week my replacement showed up, and I felt as if the world had been lifted off my shoulders. I had two regrets upon leaving this company—that I didn't get to see Mr. Bromley and that I developed high blood pressure.

Jo-Jo, Mark, and I were singing as we drove through the snow and were headed to sunny Florida. We were happy also because we would be home with our family by Christmas—even without a job.

CHAPTER 4

COCOA BEACH, NEW MEXICO AND INDIANA

1978

After a glorious holiday season with the family, I had to start beating the bushes again for a job. I began as usual by sending resumés to major hotel chains and scanning the classified ads in trade magazines and newspapers. Through a friend in the business, he gave me a lead to another guru in a young company. As I said before, "Timing is everything." It was right under my nose. The company had recently purchased the Merritt Island Holiday Inn. I got lucky by catching the owner at the property. He and Charles Clayton, the VP and comptroller, interviewed me by the swimming pool. Dwayne Davidson, CEO, excused himself to take a telephone call while Charles and I continued to talk. When Dwayne, who was extremely hyper, returned, he told Charles that they had just acquired another inn. He smiled and said, "Charles, does this guy know the hotel business?" Charles, in his serious voice and solemn look, said, "He has the experience, will relocate, but prefers Florida." Dwayne said, "In time that will be no problem. Work out the details and get Chance on board." Again, the mover and shaker excused himself. He met a blonde across the pool and they left arm in arm. Charles continued to tell me about the company known as "Double D Inns." Two brothers, Dwayne and Daniel Davidson, had inherited large farms and coal mines in the Midwest. Their holdings made excess profits so they invested in the hotel business for a writeoff. Surprisingly they began to make money. Dwayne was an Ivy League playboy, while Dan was still one of the good old boys.

Charles and I made our deal, and he said that he would contact me in two days. I was happy with the lucrative offer but had no idea where I would be assigned. Again, I was going to be an innkeeper since this is the term Holiday Inns used to refer to their general managers and Holiday Inn was the only franchise brand the company was buying. I didn't realize what was ahead.

Just as Charles had said, he called me and said that he would like for me to be in Clovis, New Mexico, within five days. I thought, "Where the hell is Clovis, New Mexico?" I kissed Jo-Jo and Mark and said good-bye again and began my westward journey. After I settled in, I would fly the family out to be with me. I left Florida on a sunny, cool spring morning and arrived at the Inn three days later. As always, I drove around the property before registering. The hotel showed bad curb appeal—unkempt landscaping, shabby grounds, and missing letters on the reader board. As I entered the lobby, I looked around and noticed that the public area was rather untidy and needed a good, old-fashioned deep cleaning. Overall, the facility was a typical full-service Holiday Inn in fair condition with a good location.

I checked in and asked for the innkeeper. He kept me waiting for a while. He finally came out and introduced himself. "Hi, Chance, I'm Larry Steiner. I'm glad to see you. Why don't you get settled? We'll meet for dinner and discuss the game plan." I worked with Larry for two weeks to learn the company's philosophy, policies, and procedures. In a couple of weeks, he was called to the corporate office. After his meeting there, he took a week's vacation.

While he was gone, I took charge. I began a complete clean-up program of the property. I had never seen a motel as dusty as this one. The guests would write their names on the furniture. What a disgrace, even though this was the sandiest state that I had ever experienced.

This was sure the Wild, Wild West. Each day as the cocktail lounge would open, I noticed a regular customer would pull up in a new Cadillac or a very expensive pickup truck. He was an Indian, dressed in Western clothes, and he always spoke to everyone. Since he looked like an interesting character, I decided to buy him a drink and find out his story. I went into the lounge, sent him a drink, and introduced myself. In turn, this big, strapping Native American put out his rough hand and said, "My name is Billy Black Eagle."

After a few drinks as we became acquainted, I asked him what he did for a living. With a hardy laugh, he said, "I'm a jeweler and part-time rancher and farmer." He continued, "*Now*—this is a great country."

I said, "A jeweler?"

Billy said he made authentic Indian jewelry—primarily turquoise and silver. He admitted that he employed mostly Mexicans to make "authentic Native American" jewelry for stores back East and in California. He also had several thousand acres on which the federal government paid him not to grow crops. It is not true that Indians can't hold their liquor. I got a buzz and had to leave Billy and his friends at 11:00 P.M. He was a lot of fun and a very interesting character.

The following day, Saturday, Chief Billy came by the inn and asked for me. I came down and met him in the lobby. He was his jolly self and did not look as if he drank all night. He asked me if I would like to ride up to Ruidoso Downs in the Captain Mountains. I had heard of Ruidoso because the richest quarter horse race in the world took place there. I asked him to give me a few minutes to check on things. Since we were slow for the weekend and I had a full staff, I felt that I could leave the property.

As we drove toward the mountains, Billy opened the cooler and the bar he had set up in his Caddy. We laughed and talked all the way, primarily about the clowns in Washington. The drive was beautiful—desert to mountains instantly. Ruidoso is a quaint little town with a gorgeous little racetrack. I was excited because I had never seen quarter horse races. When we walked through the paddock, everyone spoke to the Chief. He said that he had to see someone and pointed me to our VIP seating. I picked up a program and began handicapping the races. By the time Billy joined me, I had made my wager on the first race. Billy was speaking to everyone as he made his way to his seat while carrying four beers. As the horses broke from the post, all twelve horses were neck-and-neck to the finish. It was a fast and exciting race, except I lost (as I expected). I asked Billy about the second race. He said, "Pass on it and let's have a drink." As the third race came about, the Chief appeared to be more interested. I picked a horse, Billy smiled and said, "Hey Paleface, are you sure?"

I answered, "Of course not, Injun."

He put his large finger on the number 6 horse named Sunset Paint. As I glanced down the program, I noticed the owner was Black Eagle Stables. I'll be a son-of-a-gun, Billy was the owner! Sure enough, Sunset Paint won the race. What a day. Billy's horses won three out of five races in which they were entered. After the races, Billy took me to the Red Dog Saloon, where he introduced me to several other Indians and cowboys. The Chief showed me a great time as well as helping me win over a grand for the day. I couldn't wait to take Jo-Jo to Ruidoso. Before we left, some redneck idiot had to wise off to Billy (some off-color remark). The Chief tried to ignore the comment. The second remark resulted in a John Wayne hook to the jaw of the rude cowboy. Down he went and up popped two of his friends and down they went. It was a quick little saloon fight. As we left, the Chief laughed and said, "Isn't this great!"

The following week, my family arrived as Larry also returned. When Larry and I walked the property, I could feel that he was uncomfortable with me because of the changes that had occurred. Larry definitely could squeeze a buffalo nickel into an Indian head penny. He ran a tight ship in bringing in the bottom line while losing good innkeeping practices and spending nothing on capital improvements. This situation continued for a couple of weeks. I did have the opportunity to enjoy and show my family the great state of New Mexico. Jo-Jo, Mark, and I enjoyed Ruidoso by winning money, meeting the jockeys, and seeing the good old boys.

While I was marking time and being bored with my job, Charles called and asked me to meet him in Indiana. After managing Hiltons and Sheratons, being with a Holiday Inn franchisee was a culture shock. It appeared that the major hotel/motel companies did not care what condition the properties were maintained in as long as they receive their franchise fees.

Kemmons Wilson and his associates did a wonderful job of programming the middle-class traveling public to put their heads in the beds. They did create a great reservation system for the public. It sure was a pain in the ass when there was only one room clerk with several guests trying to check in or out and another guest wanting to make several reservations at other Holiday Inns, when all the guest had to do was call the toll-tree telephone number. At times, it appears that when some guests walk through a hotel's lobby doors, they become demanding, helpless, or just plain lazy. Like with the restaurant business, the general public expects perfection out of the hotel/motel industry or they want something for free.

I put my family on a plane in Lubbock, Texas, and I began my trip north. As I drove toward Evansville, I was happy to be away from Larry because he and I had opposite management practices. What a difference in properties—from an older, standard Holiday Inn to a new Holidome property. This was more my style. This hotel was only a few months old but needed aggressive marketing and management. The architectural design was uniquely different than anything I had seen. The open-air dome had a replica of a riverboat to the entrance of the restaurant. One side of the inside building was painted and designed as a small town. The two-hundred-room hotel had a beautifully appointed lounge and meeting rooms. Since the property was new, it was in excellent condition and the staff appeared competent, but the hotel was not doing the dollars the owner expected. With my experience, Dwayne and Charles expected me to increase revenues.

I went back to basics as taught to me by Mr. Bromley—learn the market, and write and execute a business plan. I hired a salesperson, learned the market, and studied the competition. This industrial city needed a good hotel as the in spot. I sent our sales manager out knocking on doors (ten sales calls per day). I began to create promotions for our food and beverage outlets. We installed an advertisement program to entice the public to use our services. This was the fun part of the business. I dug up some of the old gimmicks such as the romantic rendezvous package, ladies night, holiday specials, "deal with a wheel," dance contests, jam sessions, VIP drawings, guest of the day program, an elegant Sunday brunch, a secretary's club, and my favorite—The Gong Show. This promotion took place on Thursday nights in the lounge. I studied the TV "Gong Show" and tried to emulate Chuckie. Jo-Jo opened the show and introduced me as the host. She also assembled my wardrobe, including tuxedos, crazy shirts, and hats. We had a unique panel of judges—the county sheriff, the most popular DJs or entertainers in town, and a guest from the media or the mayor's office. They used a plunger and a garbage can lid as their gonger. We had no problem acquiring judges since they drank free (especially the sheriff or politicians). We began giving a hundred-dollar bill to the winner and other prizes to all participants who did not get gonged. My food and beverage director was a rugged, handsome Italian, John Sputo, who was crazy and had a great sense of humor. He was the Unknown Comic and Gene, Gene, the Dancing Machine. With Jo-Jo's help and the house band, the show became an instant hit. The lounge was grossing between $150 and $200 a day, and after three weeks we would do over $3,000 every Thursday. Not only did we have good singers, musicians, bands, comics, dancers, and magicians, but we enjoyed hog callers, spoon players (even some with their own teeth), knee knockers, jugglers, belly dancers, acrobats, baton twirlers, and one piccolo player! Our customers were coming from surrounding counties, and the lounge would fill to its capacity of over five hundred persons. Dwayne, Dan, and Charles could not believe the response of the public to this insane promotion. Charles asked me to put the show together for five other Holiday Inns in the Midwest. I put him on hold so that I could finish the year with the final grand-prize-winner show. He agreed.

Since our owners partied as hard as they worked, John and I did as well. Before the final three weeks, Jo-Jo was called to England due to family illness. I truly missed her, so John became my drinking buddy. Again I fell in the habit of cocktails every day. Before the last two shows, John and I were planning the shows, Dwayne called me to the executive suite. He informed me that the suite bar needed to be stocked. When John and I arrived at the suite, Dwayne said, "Come on in and join the party." He had

Sandy, Kathy, and Barbara in the room—two cocktail waitresses and a front-desk clerk. Barbara was in the hot tub with Dwayne while the other two were sitting at the bar. All together they shouted, "Surprise." The girls mixed everyone a drink and said, "Hey Boss, relax, have a drink and let's have some fun before work." Again, after always being a leader, I was easily influenced by a drinking buddy, Wild Turkey, and a pretty trollop. Again, I justified my actions because my boss, the CEO of the company, insisted my right-hand man and myself should party with him. When I left the suite, I thought, "What the hell have I done again—disrespect to Jo-Jo, myself, and my family while losing all I wanted from my staff—respect!"

I checked in with my MOD, drank a steaming cup of black coffee, freshened up, and collected myself. As usual, a very large crowd had gathered in the lounge for The Gong Show. The show was moving along at its usual fast pace when I introduced the Unknown Comic (John). When John tried to jump on the stage, he missed and fell. I made a joke, cut the lights, and took a break. The crowd went wild with laughter. They did not know that it was not part of the act. I went backstage—John was drunk as a skunk, still with the paper bag on his head, while his ankle began to swell. He said, "Boss, I'm sorry, but I can go on. I won't let you down." I said no but he insisted. I opened the second part of the show with the Unknown Comic—in a wheelchair. The audience began to laugh again as John rolled into the spotlight. He began with one of his funniest jokes: "My wife and I have two of the most beautiful and perfect daughters in the world. But I did want a son. After visiting my wife in the hospital, I went down the hall to the nursery to see our son—God, was he ugly! The tiny guy looked like a little, bald, red monkey! I stomped back to the wife's room and asked, 'Did you have an affair? That can't be mine.' She smiled and said, 'Not this time.'"

John was at his comical best. After the show I took John to the emergency room at the general hospital. After an exam and X rays, the doctor came out and informed us that John had broken his ankle. He had a cast put on his leg. We stopped for a nightcap and laughed about the events of the last twenty-four hours. At the end of year and the final show we had standing-room-only with a record day's business. In January, we received a call and a letter from the network that produced "The Gong Show." They informed us that we were in violation of their copyright and we must stop. I felt honored that a major network was concerned about our little show. We ceased putting on the show for a couple of months and renamed it the "Super Pong Show." Since the public knew of the promotion, it continued to be as successful as before.

Charles called me to his office for the annual review of the property and of me. I didn't know what to expect because they would fire a manager at the drop of a hat and seldom gave a reason. After a favorable financial review, Charles asked me to oversee, audit, and market the other five Midwest properties. He expected me to manage my property as well as the other duties, for an insignificant raise. Because of ego reasons, I agreed. This doubled my workload and responsibilities—which later led to my continued high blood pressure condition! This promotion also created a very stressful situation at home, because I was gone three or four days per week.

After the second bone-chilling Midwestern winter, Jo-Jo and Mark went back to Florida. I did take my family for granted and lost my perception of what was important in life. I continued to work extremely hard and play at the same pace. At times I missed the family, especially when I went home by myself. I stayed busy so I wouldn't think about my emptiness.

One Wednesday afternoon I was walking the property and the front office paged me. As I approached the font desk, a middle-aged man sporting a crew cut and a short-sleeved white shirt with matching white socks stopped me. He introduced himself as the Holiday Inn Quality Assurance Inspector. He had his little pad and checklists ready. Since we were a new hotel with a good staff, I knew that we would score very high. My front office manager handed us a list of vacant and ready rooms to inspect. As we headed to the first vacant room, he peeled off into a room where a housekeeper was working. He began questioning the young lady (who could barely speak English). Juanita, who had joined the staff only two weeks previous, became very nervous. I grabbed Johnson by his elbow and asked, "What the hell are you doing?"

He replied, "My job by finding out how well the employees know their job and Holiday Inn policies."

In a loud voice, I said, "And that's my job not yours. You can inspect the physical property, write your report, and leave. Do you forget that we franchisees pay your salary?"

In a military fashion he replied, "No, sir!"

When he finished his inspection and we reviewed the report, I was not happy. As we talked, I asked, "What did you do before joining Holiday Inns?"

Johnson proudly answered, "I was in the military and coached football."

I smiled and said, "That sure qualifies you to inspect and advise us how to run a hotel." I refused to sign the inspection report due to unfair remarks concerning housekeeping. My executive housekeeper, Maria, was very detailed and meticulous, and she had won industry awards. The hotel had only one complaint in the past eight months. As I waved bye to Johnson, I wondered where corporations get these guys? Relatives, friends, who they knew . . .

Even though I lived under pressure, the guys treated me very well and enjoyed having me party with them. Once, Dwayne and Charles called me from the airport and asked me to fly with them to Las Vegas in their private plane. When we arrived at the Stardust Resort, everyone jumped when they saw the Davidsons. We all had complimentary suites, food, and beverage, and even hookers were on call. I did enjoy the gaming tables and was impressed with the glamour, but I felt guilty all the time that I was in Sin City. After three days we went home with hangovers and back to work as normal.

Again I was working for another strange corporation with eccentric owners. On one occasion, Dwayne called me from his car phone to tell me that he needed the executive suite that evening. I explained that it was booked for the guest speaker, Senator Ford, for the next day's conference. Before he could say anything, I told him the other VIP suite was booked for the vice president of the railroad (we had a lucrative annual contract with the railroad). Dwayne interrupted me and said that he didn't care who was coming in, get the executive suite ready for him! So I met with my front office manager and rearranged the assigned rooms. I put Mr. Swain, the railroad executive, in a mini-suite with a complimentary fruit basket and champagne. Later that evening Dwayne arrived in his new white Excalibur with an absolutely gorgeous woman. He paraded into the lounge with her on his arm and came up to the bar where John and I were sitting. He introduced Tiffany to us and let us know that she was the Playmate for the month of June. Then in his snappy tone, he asked if I had his key to the suite. I passed it to him. He left while John and I ordered another cocktail.

The next morning Charles gave me a call and told me that I needed to go to St. Louis and terminate Alex, the food and beverage director. I questioned why the innkeeper, Anne, could not handle the task. He continued by telling me to put her on warning. As usual, I did as I was told and drove toward the property. While driving, I began soul searching. When I arrived at the inn, all looked normal. It was about 8:00 P.M. and the restaurant and lounge still appeared quite busy. Upon entering the restaurant, I noticed Alex was working the front. He was a handsome, friendly young man in his early thirties. Alex greeted me and with a big smile asked if I would like a table. I said no thanks, that I would go check in and see him later. Later that evening I went into the lounge for a nightcap and spoke to Ron the bartender. As I sipped my drink, Ron began to chew my ear while I just wanted a little quiet time.

But what I learned from the bartender proved to be very interesting. Ron passed along the latest gossip of the hotel. Kim, a pretty little cocktail waitress, dated Mr. Dwayne Davidson when he was in town. But then she broke it off and refused to see Dwayne over the past two months. Ron continued with his story by telling me that Kim gave her notice and she and Alex were planning their wedding. I left and went to my room to sleep on this situation.

The next morning, I arose early and took a walk to organize my thoughts for my upcoming meetings. Even though I was down early, Anne and Alex were waiting for me with a cup of coffee. I met with both of them behind closed doors and advised them that I knew what the deal was. I advised Alex to resign with a letter of recommendation from me because the "boys" would make it very difficult for him. I advised Anne to "watch her back." I wished them good luck and left the inn. I didn't tell them that I was there as a hatchet man to terminate Alex.

As I drove back to Evansville, I decided that I had to get away from these guys. I went home to call Jo-Jo to tell her my love for her and ask for her forgiveness. I told her that after the annual managers' meeting in December I would resign and leave immediately to come home to Florida.

As expected, there was no mention of bonuses or raises at the managers' meeting. Just tougher budgets for the coming year. I had my two-week notice of resignation letter ready and handed it to Charles at the close of the second day. He appeared shocked and surprised as he said, "Fine," and walked away. These guys could not stand for anyone to leave them. Charles turned around and said, "Chance, you can leave now!" I left the meeting, went to Evansville, packed, and headed south. Again, I felt totally relieved. As I drove to Florida, I thought, "This is beginning to become a habit." Again I gave up another lucrative position for peace of mind, stress reduction, and happiness. As mentioned before, each inn had its own personality while each company had its own character—good or bad, positive or negative!

The seventies introduced us to bar codes, unleaded gas, airbags, and digital watches. Science created an artificial heart and we explored the heavens with Skylab, Mariner, and Voyager. The world's tallest buildings—New York's World Trade Center Towers and Chicago's Sears' Tower—were built. We received bad news with the loss of Louis Armstrong and Elvis Presley and the introduction of a new virus known as AIDS. Hollywood gave us *Jaws, Star Wars,* and *Saturday Night Fever,* while New York provided *Saturday Night Live*!

The Miami Dolphins and the Pittsburgh Steelers dominated football, while three great heavyweight champions—George Foreman, Joe Frazier, and Muhammad Ali—beat up each other. The Vietnam War ended! America continued to breakdance in the discos to the sounds of KC and the Sunshine Band. Men were fashionable in their bell-bottom pants and platform shoes while they were admiring the chicks wearing hot pants and miniskirts. I became a father, separated and was forgiven, was rich and broke, overcame an alcohol problem, and was used by friends. My family stuck by me. I lost a motel, traveled extensively, and gave up two good positions, but what a ride in this decade!

While reminiscing, I continued speeding down the highway toward Florida. I quickly came back to reality when a state trooper pulled me over. This was another strange experience. The overweight, sarcastic officer told me to follow him. Since it was late in the night, I wondered where we were going. In a few moments we arrived at a truck weighing station, and the trooper escorted me into the back office of the facility. Upon entering, I saw several other people sitting in the small room. The officer announced that the Justice of the Peace would arrive very shortly. While looking around the room, I wondered if this was going to be a kangaroo court. A few minutes passed and in walked a huge, red-faced older gentleman tugging at his black robe. In an instant, he said, "Everyone stand and swear after me." We all repeated to tell the truth and nothing but the truth. He continued by saying, "I'm the Honorable Horace Smith and will be presiding over this traffic court." Some of the defendants were held over while the ones with cash were released. I was thankful that I had cashed a check before leaving Indiana. I pleaded guilty and paid a seventy-five-dollar cash fine. I did not get a receipt, and I was very happy to leave the bizarre place. When I made it to Florida, I called the FBI office to report the racket set up in the name of the law.

I decided to stop in Jacksonville Beach to see my friend Bob Nelson, executive director of the Chamber of Commerce. We had lunch and I left my resumé with Bob because he knew everyone. He informed me that major changes were coming for the beach hotels. Bob asked me to be his guest for the night, but I thanked him and declined.

I was very anxious to continue down I-95 to Cocoa Beach to see my Jo-Jo and Mark.

CHAPTER 5

JACKSONVILLE BEACH

1980

After being unemployed for two months, completing all my "Honey-Do" lists, enjoying the beach, and fishing, I received a call from Jack Ahern, president of REMCO (Real Estate Management Corporation). He asked, "Chance Wayne, did you operate the Sheraton Beach Resort?"

I sharply answered, "Yes, sir."

Mr. Ahern continued by informing me that his company had assumed the paper and the management of the property. The gentleman said that he met with Bob Nelson, who passed along my resumé. He said Bob spoke very highly of me. Mr. Ahern asked me to meet him at the property day after tomorrow (Saturday), and of course I excitedly agreed.

Jo-Jo had my favorite Hart, Schaffner and Marx interview suit ready at all times. As usual, I arrived early in order to have a look at the property. It was disappointing to see how such a beautiful hotel had been neglected in the past five years. The lush, tropical landscaping needed care as did the entrance and the lobby. I informed the front-desk clerk that I would be waiting for Mr. Ahern in the restaurant. In a few minutes, a handsome, distinguished gentleman in his early forties came over to me and introduced himself. I said, "It is a pleasure to meet you, Mr. Ahern."

Immediately, he replied, "Chance, call me Jack." He continued by telling me about his background in banking, finance, and real estate. He said that he had formed several real estate trusts and that the Sheraton was part of one portfolio. During my unconventional interview, I began to feel very comfortable and gained respect for Jack. He said one thing that I truly appreciated: "Everyone thinks they can run a hotel. I quickly learned that I needed an experienced, dedicated hotel manager. Hotels are different from all other real estate investments because they need attention twenty-four hours a day." He offered me a lucrative package that included living on property if we chose to do so. As the conversation continued, Jack said that he would like for me to take over on Monday. He told me that he expected me to run the property as if it was mine. In his sharp clean voice Jack said, "I would like to have dinner with you and your family." He was a mover and shaker, just as I liked to think of myself. Since I was used to these types of individuals, I agreed. I liked his style. I called Jo-Jo and told her of our latest adventure. As usual, trouper that she was, Jo-Jo organized us and we were on the road again.

SOP (Standard Operating Procedure) again: review property, staff meetings, write a business/marketing plan, budgets, policies and procedures, employee handbook, review financial statements and expenses, personnel review, etc. After getting through the basics, I called my old friends, the three Bobs—Nelson, Atkinson, and O'Neil. We met at the Turtle Inn to tip a few for old times' sake. The guys brought me up to date with all the activities in the area. The PGA established new championship golf courses in Ponte Vedra at Sawgrass, Mayport Naval Base expanded, downtown Jacksonville was redeveloped, bids were submitted for an NFL franchise, an international airport, and numerous other economic developments. Since I knew the area, I became excited with the possibility of investments.

I presented Mr. Ahern the budgets for capital improvements and operations. After a couple of questions, he approved both proposals. I immediately began getting bids for the refurbishment of the hotel. After finding out who the team players were, I released the sales director, the executive housekeeper, and the evening chef. The just causes were undermining and resisting changes in new policies and procedures. I never liked for anyone to say, "Well, we have always done it that way." When the executive housekeeper left, she took four housekeepers with her—two were relatives. That same evening we had a threatening telephone call about getting even by blowing up the hotel. I reassured Jo-Jo that nothing was going to happen because I had heard those types of threats before.

There was one bad scene when the rude redneck gang left, I wasn't worried. On Friday night when the hotel was packed, including the lounge and restaurant with our "TGIF" crowd, the front-desk manager, David, received a telephone call from a garbled voice saying that there was a bomb in the hotel. David immediately located me and informed me of the terrifying message. I told him to be calm, don't speak to anyone, and that I was on the way to the front desk. Even though David was the MOD, he was rather hyper and was acting like an expectant father. I called him into my office and had him repeat the precise message. I in turn called Pete Meyers, the chief of police. He told me to evacuate the hotel. After hanging up from Pete, I stopped and thought for a moment. Since the hotel was full, I decided to pull the fire alarm. I called my family and my security guard, Clyde Dobson, to inform them of the situation. The evacuation went rather orderly—David helped at the front lobby doors, Clyde cleared the public areas and kitchen, while I ran the hallways and knocked on all room doors. All of a sudden, the hotel parking lot looked and sounded like World War II. Police, firemen, the bomb squad, ambulances, and the media were scampering everywhere. The police bomb squad with their dogs came in like gangbusters. I greeted them and advised them of the situation. I told them that I thought the hotel had been emptied. They informed me that they would handle it from here. While the guests filled the parking lots, my staff, Jo-Jo and I mingled with the guests. Clyde and I retrieved the portable bar from the pool deck and offered cocktails to the guests and media.

Overall, everyone was understanding and kind—except for a couple of jerks. Even some of our regular customers said they were leaving and for us to bill them for what they owed. The media was tracking me like a pack of Georgia bloodhounds. I continued to tell them, "No comment at this time." After a couple of hours, the chief called me over and interviewed me. I informed him of the events that had occurred over the past few weeks. He said that he thinks that it was a hoax and that the squads had searched the property thoroughly. He gave the all-clear signal and I advised the guests of the situation. I sent Jo-Jo and Mark over to our friends, Joe and Ginger's. I then led the crowd back into the hotel. I bought everyone in the restaurant and lounge a drink and thanked everyone for being understanding. I bought Tom, the bartender, and myself a drink. After a couple of hours when I thought it was truly safe, I called Jo-Jo and asked her to bring our friends for a nightcap. We had a few cocktails as well as many laughs. It appeared all ended well in another interesting day at the hotel.

Every morning, I look in the mirror, smile, take a big deep breath, and remember—attitude is everything in life. I arrived at the hotel the next day, got my morning coffee, and reviewed the daily report. In a few moments I overheard a very unhappy guest screaming at David. David met me in the hall as I was headed toward the front desk. Mrs. Albright demanded a free stay. David agreed for one night but she wanted the entire stay—five nights! I told Mrs. Albright absolutely not. She continued by saying that everyone had been rude and her room had never been cleaned properly. We apologized and went on with our work. Mrs. Albright headed toward the dining room. I told David that's not the last we will hear from her. Sure enough within an hour, the dining room hostess (Diane) called for me. Diane said Mrs. Albright said she waited too long for her breakfast, which was not cooked properly (but she ate the entire meal), and she was ignored. I calmed Diane, the waitress, and Mrs. Albright. I apologized to her, picked up her check, and tipped the waitress out of my pocket. I went back to work. A couple hours later, Mrs. Albright called the desk and complained about the housekeeper. Alice was one of our nicest and sweetest employees. Mrs. Albright said she was awakened by the housekeeper. No "Do Not Disturb" sign was out and Alice had tried to clean the room. I called Mrs. Albright to ask if she needed housekeeping and, if not, to please put out the sign. She put the sign out. This was about 2:30 P.M. Now at 5:30 P.M., Mrs. Albright called and was complaining that she had not received any service. David apologized and sent her towels. Again, the next morning Mrs. Albright began demanding a free room and wanting to extend her stay. I interrupted and she began to raise her voice while she was inches from my face. I said, "Ma'am, I will be right around to see you!" As I walked around the front desk, I took off my suit jacket and I said, "Mrs. Albright, follow me." I laid my jacket down in front of the lobby door, laid down on it and said in a loud voice, "Now, walk over me as you have done my entire staff!" Her mouth fell open; she shook her head and hurried toward the elevator. Within an hour, Mrs. Albright checked out. My staff applauded.

During the next few months, working with a close capital budget, the hotel received a new facelift. After my new executive housekeeper, Mary Ellen, completed a thorough deep-cleaning program, we were proud of the property. With our aggressive marketing plan in place, business began to increase. The Golden Pelican and Bogie's were busy again with their previous customers. Even though I began to notice that the work force was becoming less effective and less productive (just plain lazy), I did assemble an adequate staff. I began to have more leisure time—that's when I would get ambitious and Jo-Jo would become nervous.

A friend, Jake Howard, presented me with a proposition to invest in a restaurant (The Tele-Deli). It was located in The Southern Bell Telephone Building. The numbers looked good due to being a built-in business. It only served breakfast and lunch and opened five days a week (no weekends or holidays). This worked fine for several months until Jake ran off with a telephone operator. This put me in a real bind but, as usual, Jo-Jo stepped in and took over the restaurant. She cleaned it up and operated it better than ever before. The clientele and staff loved Jo-Jo. Of course, being a trusting soul as I was, Jake emptied the cash out of the bank, took an extra loan, and left us with a great deal of unpaid bills. I set up an appointment with John Tate of the Small Business Administration (SBA). For a government official, John was an honest gentleman. I told him of our situation and our experience and presented him our excellent personal finances with references.

John reviewed our package and said, "Chance, if I was a bank loan officer, I would give you the loan this moment. I will give you this oversize, thick application but you are wasting your time and mine."

I said, "Why?"

He continued by telling me that he was taking an early retirement in three weeks because of the unfair system of the government. He said, "Chance, I know you and Mrs. Wayne would repay the loan without a doubt. I will help complete the application and send it to the right source. *But* the loan will not be approved because you are not in a minority. This is the main reason that I am leaving the service. Our government does not treat all citizens equally, particularly the middle-class white male. My brother-in-law went through the same exercise with no success, even with my help!" I thanked John and invited him and his wife to the restaurant. Another interesting experience dealing with the "people's government."

While Jo-Jo continued to run our restaurant and raise Mark, I continued to build the business at the hotel. Again with the help of my staff, we were again the in spot of the beach. Jo-Jo and I purchased a beautiful townhouse in Ponte Vedra. Again we were living "high on the hog."

One Friday afternoon while I was at the front desk, a shapely lady in her late thirties came to the desk and asked for another key to her room. This was not unusual but a regular request. What was unusual was the color of the guest's hair—bright green! It did go well with her cute little orange bikini. The Sixties and Seventies had brought in some bizarre fads, but I felt that our swimming pool had produced the enchanting color. David and I did laugh to ourselves, but I immediately called the maintenance chief to meet me by the pool. Joe and I took the readings of the pool and wow! The chemical balance was totally off the scale. Even though the guest was a beautiful bleached blonde that would swim and then bake under the broiling sun, I felt liable. I told Joe to close the pool and administer a shock treatment.

When I arrived back at the front desk, I asked, "David, have you heard from the green-haired lady?"

He laughed and said, "Not yet."

Within minutes, I heard the guest in question screaming and cursing at David. I went to his rescue. I said, "Ma'am, may I help you?"

She replied, "You can if you can restore my hair to its blonde color!" She continued, "You bastards saw the color when I came for my key and neither of you said anything!"

I acknowledged, "You are right, ma'am, but we do have theatrical groups and clowns in the hotel."

She blasted me, "Are you calling me a f—— clown?"

"Oh no, ma'am, not a stunning beauty of your quality." Before she could reply, I offered a complete beauty treatment, dinner for two, and a complimentary night's stay. She agreed if I would join her later for cocktails. The deal was made.

As life's pathway offers hills and dales, so does the life of a hotel manager. Except for the bomb scare, the past year was rather uneventful. The following year provided several exciting events. First, Hurricane David decided to show nature's powerful force to the east coast of Florida. As always, we received sufficient time to prepare for the awesome impact of this storm. Plywood, sandbags, flashlights, batteries, water (sounds silly), canned food, candles, gas in automobiles, and an evacuation plan for the hotel was standard operating procedure for such disasters. As David approached, the emergency agency ordered a complete evacuation of the beach area. The maintenance men secured the building, installed plywood over the first floor's plate glass doors and windows. We did not put plywood on the other seven floors. We planted sandbags throughout the perimeter of the hotel. We put all the pool and patio furniture into the swimming pool. We checked the generators as well as all battery backup items. We turned off everything possible. When I felt the hotel was as secure as possible, I sent the balance of the staff home. I insisted that Jo-Jo go inland to stay at our friends' home. She insisted that she would stay with me. We sent Mark to stay with his grandparents. Jo-Jo and I made certain without a doubt that no one else was in the hotel. It was very, very, very eerie and quiet for a while. We made ourselves comfortable with our supplies in the apartment and waited for the big blow. The afternoon grew darker and darker. The rain came heavier. The winds increased to sixty miles per hour. The waves showed their whitecaps at five to six feet high. The lightning and thunder became louder and closer as night was upon us.

As the night continued, the storm became more intense. At its peak, it sounded like a very long, long freight train passing outside our window. It continued to be noisy for several hours. It never quieted, which meant the eye never passed over us. We did hear an earth-shattering crash of glass. Against Jo-Jo's advice, I went to our balcony to see if I could see the damage. I could not see anything, but I damn near got blown off the balcony. We settled in and snuggled up for the remainder of the night. As sunrise approached, the sounds of nature subsided except for a steady rainfall.

When daylight arrived, Jo-Jo and I were anxious to go out and survey the damage. As we unlocked the front doors, water was up to the sandbags. As we stepped into the water, it appeared that we were now in a flood situation. There were large palm trees uprooted, one automobile overturned, signs blown down, and pieces of roofs in the streets. Highway A1A looked like a small river with tree limbs everywhere, and that was just in front of the hotel. We made our way around the hotel through the steady precipitation. The ocean side revealed that the beach had disappeared. A palm tree was leaning against the hotel, water up to the patios and a broken sliding glass door. This was the loud crash we heard, which was only two doors down from the apartment.

We went back inside to check each floor and the equipment. We discovered a few leaks and, of course, we had no electricity. By afternoon, the sun was trying to break through the overcast. The rain began to slow and on came the electricity. Some streets were still flooded but draining rapidly. Joe, my maintenance chief, and his family came in and asked if we were okay. The ladies went to the kitchen to prepare us a large dinner while Joe and I continued to secure and clean up the hotel.

The next day some of the staff reported to work while a few reservations also checked in. After a good cleaning of the hotel and the clean-up of the city, within a few days business continued as usual.

I began to put pressure on the sales department to create more banquet revenue. As this area increased, parking became a problem. To solve this situation, I set up a valet service. This went well until Frankie, a cocky young hustler, decided to take a little joyride in a new Porsche. The only thing wrong—it did not belong to Frankie! The owner was Hank Dickerson, a friend and a very good customer. Hank was a local, wealthy real estate developer and all-around good guy. As Hank and I observed human behavior at the reception, we simultaneously noticed a common practice. A CEO and a few young people in their twenties were gathered by the hors d'oeuvre table. An older lady, the server, was trying to replace an empty tray.

The young business persons turned and looked right through the hard-working little woman. They rudely turned around and continued their conversation. At that point, Hank and I walked over and asked the crowd to move in order that the lady could continue her job. She smiled and thanked us. Everyone deserves respect.

When Hank went to retrieve his sporty vehicle, George, the other valet, said that he could not find the automobile. Just at that time, up came a fast-driving Frankie. The speedy-talking young man jumped out of the car as if nothing was wrong. Hank was a very astute man. He popped his head inside his automobile and looked at the odometer. Hank roared back at Frankie and said, "Where the hell have you been in my car?"

Frankie began to stutter and said "I just. . . ."

Hank screamed again, "A scratch!"

Frankie began to run as Hank headed toward him. Hank came into the hotel to see me. I bought Hank a drink as he began to settle down. Hank filed his claim with his insurance company, and I never saw Frankie again.

Speaking of human behavior, the piano bar in Bogie's Lounge was a great place to observe action and reaction. It always appeared that the piano bar drew mature women like a magnet. I contracted a middle-aged, handsome Italian piano player/singer who charmed the pants off the women. Of course, in turn the women drew the lounge lizards. Ginger, a friend of Jo-Jo, told me how lounge lizards operate. She said, "They are slick, smooth-tongued devils that slide from lounge to lounge trying to pick up anyone who would have them."

A couple of months later, my crazy buddy, Bargain Bob, who owned a local sports store, called me to set up a meeting. I thought, "What is he up to now?" Bob and I met one afternoon for a drinking meeting. By the time we finished, Bob had talked me into thinking about a boxing promotion. He told me that he had a chance to set up and promote a heavyweight fight and a training camp for light-heavyweight champion, Matthew Saad Mohammed. After clearing my head the next morning, I kept going back to Bob's proposition. I reviewed the function banquet book and found that we did not have much booked at that particular time of the year. Bob wanted to set up the hotel's convention center as a training camp for the Champ and his fighter Jody Ballard, a ranked heavyweight. I called Bob for another meeting. He laid out his plan and offered me a 50-50 partnership. The plan:

Set up amateur fights for a one-night program—Receive ticket sales.

Set up training camp for the Champ—Charge to see training sessions.

Set up pro fights with the main event between two ranked heavyweights—Jody Ballard vs. Leon Shaw to be held at Jacksonville Coliseum.

Set up press conferences at the Sheraton Beach Resort.

I agreed because it looked profitable for all parties involved, including the hotel! Bob made the deal with the Champ's manager and signed Jody and Leon for their fight. Everything began to fall into place. We set up a press conference at the hotel, which was attended by all the media—newspapers, TV, and radio. We then began to advertise for fighters as well as promote all the fights. Jody

Ballard was in Matthew's camp as a sparring partner and for his own training.

The hotel was the talk of the town with all the free publicity. Room, food, and beverage sales increased sharply. Rumors of a visit from Muhammad Ali to wish Matthew success against Dwight Braxton brought even more attention to the hotel. Matthew and Muhammad were both gentlemen as were their entourages. The only major problem Bob and I ran into was finding the proper-sized ring in Jacksonville.

We held the amateur fights in the hotel ballroom and sold out (eight hundred people). We had an excellent fight card, with good fighters of all weight classes from Florida, Georgia, and North Carolina. Bob and I made a nice profit from the amateur fights and thought we were big-time promoters. The training camp was going very well, so we called another press conference at the Sheraton. Another good turnout by all the media. We had Matthew as the guest of honor to comment on his upcoming fight. We introduced Jody and Leon to comment on their upcoming fight. Everything was going well, even as Bob (he thought he was Don King) stirred up both fighters and offered an extra two thousand dollars for a knockout!

One Wednesday afternoon (a week before the fight) Crazy Bob picked me up at the hotel and said we had to find round girls. He took me to the Babes House and Bob began to act like a Hollywood producer, flashing hundred-dollar bills and buying drinks. He called over a gorgeous, tall blonde and put a fifty-dollar bill in her bra. Bob began with his smooth line of blarney, and we had a ring girl. He wasn't satisfied. He wanted another. If I had not dragged him out of the joint, we may have had a dozen ring girls.

Fight night came. A fair crowd—several hundred, not several thousand—showed up for the first (and last) of the Friday night fights! The preliminary fights were very tense and exciting. The main event ended in the first round with Leon winning by a knockout! At the end of the next day, we settled up, and we had lost our asses! End of my life as a promoter—back to being a hotel manager. Bob and I are still friends. Matthew lost his belt to Braxton. Another costly and exciting experience. Jo-Jo finally began to speak to me again.

As the months passed, Bob Nelson had me involved in everything—on the board of the Tourist and Convention Bureau, officer in the Hotel/Motel Association, the Toastmasters, the Kiwanis, the Navy League, Ducks Unlimited, and the Board of the Chamber of Commerce. He suggested that I run for public office. The other Bob (O'Neill) was mayor of Jacksonville Beach as well as a hotel manager. We all would meet for our weekly "solve the world problems" cocktail meeting. We began the Resort Tax (1 percent), also known as the "Bed Tax" for the sole purpose of promoting the area. As time passed, the politicians took charge of the funds and began to find other uses for the taxes. Periodically they would increase the tax, and the hotels served as their tax collectors. It appeared that we were defeating the original objective of this vote. I had to stop and take stock of my situation, which made me realize that I was spending too much time in community affairs and not enough quality time in the hotel and with my family.

I began to resign from each organization/association and concentrate on operating the hotel and selling the Tele-Deli. The only activities and meetings that I would attend were the ones that could help the hotel and restaurant. I met a nice black man named Henry Thompson who worked for the city of Jacksonville. As we chatted, I asked him if he knew someone that would be interested in purchasing the Tele-Deli. His big dark eyes lit up; he let out a hearty laugh and said, "I sure do, me! I have an SBA loan pending, and this fits the bill perfectly." He continued, "I have always wanted to own a restaurant." I gave Henry a price and without a counteroffer or hesitation he agreed. Even though Jo-Jo and I were qualified with experience for an SBA loan and Mr. Thompson did not, we got SBA money indirectly.

Even though I had an efficient and loyal staff, while spending too much time away from the hotel, the property became lax. Since my boss was a hard-ass, I felt that I had better get into the swing. I went back to inspecting all departments and detail inspections of the rooms and public areas. Since Jo-Jo was my biggest critic, at times I would ask her to walk through the property. I also contracted shoppers to review the total property periodically.

Most hotels had a policy of not hiring relatives in the same department or not at all. We had the same policy but as all rules are made to be broken, we had a mother/daughter, two sisters, and an aunt working in housekeeping. I didn't know this had happened—shame on me. Also, I didn't know that this clique dominated the department. I did question why we continuously lost housekeepers. I met with Mary Ellen and told her that we had to break up the bullies. Mary Ellen was a fine, upright, quiet lady in her forties. She didn't like upsetting anyone, so I went in as the bad guy. I revised the schedule and cut hours. When the schedule was posted, the troops came marching up to my office and demanded the days to work they had chosen. I reminded the ladies that I managed the hotel, Mary Ellen ran the housekeeping department, and each one of them were employees, not supervisors. I further advised them if they were not happy being employed at the Sheraton, this is America, and they should pursue happiness elsewhere. The trouble-making five left my office cursing and slinging threats. The mother and daughter left work without saying anything to Mary Ellen. That evening, while having dinner with Jo-Jo and the Lords, I said that I hope I didn't cut my nose off to spite my face with the Fourth of July weekend coming up.

The next day, I received a strange threatening call from Big Doris's (the leader of the bullies) husband. That's when I asked my secretary, Donna, to screen all my calls. She continued to receive hang-ups. As Mary Ellen and I expected, four of the five did not show up to work with a full house on July 4. All was going well until about 2:00 A.M. The fire alarm system went off throughout the entire hotel. The family and I stayed over for the weekend due to a short staff and I was the MOD. Jo-Jo took Mark and helped the guests down the stairs to exit the building. I began to run all eight floors to ensure all the guests were out of their rooms and then headed toward the stairwells (elevators were shut down automatically). As I ran the floors, I noticed that each floor had some thick gray smoke flowing from around each laundry chute. Feeling confident that all guests were out of the building, I ran through the downstairs public area. The smoke began to get thick as I passed the laundry. Before I could get out of the building, the firemen arrived. They thundered into the hotel like a herd of buffalo as one shouted at me, "What are you doing in here?" Without thinking, I shouted, "It's my hotel and I'm doing your job!" I had been overcome with smoke and was coughing intensely. The fireman quickly responded and gave me his oxygen. While he was helping me out, I was trying to apologize for my remark. He assisted me to the ambulance and ordered me to the hospital. Jo-Jo jumped into the emergency vehicle with me. I continued to have a problem breathing because of the intense coughing. The hospital admitted me with a serious case of smoke inhalation. When we left the hotel, I thought if only the holiday tourists could see themselves—in their underwear, robes, curlers, face masks, fuzzy slippers, funny shorts with the items they grabbed. While in the ambulance with a spinning head, I thought that must be a comical scene.

The next morning, I asked for a telephone in order to find out what was going on and the status of the hotel. All the guests were fine, with some asking for a refund. The hotel suffered serious smoke damage. The fire inspector advised me that a couple of cigarettes in a laundry cart started the fire. I called Donna to pull the personnel files and advise the fire inspector of the recent events. As in all fires, a thorough investigation was conducted to determine the cause.

After the fire department released the area of the hotel, we began a thorough clean-up of the property. It was a major task to remove the smoke odor. One good outcome of this ordeal was that I quit smoking. Since we were oceanfront, at times we would open all the windows and doors of the property. After a few months passed and business returned to normal, Mr. Ahern called to arrange a luncheon meeting. I knew something was happening.

As usual, Mr. Ahern was his charming self when he informed me the hotel had been sold. I smiled and said, "This is becoming a habit." Mr. Ahern said, "Chance, I'm glad you're not upset. You did a great job, and I have another challenge for you." He continued by laying out his new plans. He offered me the opportunity of converting the Main Gate Rodeway Inn (one mile from Disney World) into a time-share operation—The Magic Tree Resort. I thought, "What the hell do I know about time sharing?" He said that if I would take the assignment he wanted me to get a real estate license and that the company would pay the expenses incurred. I thought that I would enjoy furthering my education and getting another raise as well as being in central Florida. We agreed on the terms of the deal and again I formulated a plan for the close-out of the hotel. As I drove home to inform Jo-Jo, I thought to myself that I had worked myself out of another comfortable position. As usual Jo was very supportive and we began to plan for another move. She made arrangements to sell our townhouse (as it was, including ashtrays) to a golf fanatic union official—for cash! We finished closing on the restaurant, thanks to Uncle Sam. I closed out the hotel, and the staff threw me a big going-away party. We partied and said good-bye to all our friends, again. This time, we left town with a pocket full of money and singing as Jo-Jo, Mark, and I headed to Disney World.

CHAPTER 6

KISSIMMEE, FLORIDA

1982

This time we had settled into the manager's apartment at the Main Gate Rodeway Inn. The conversion of the motel into a time-share operation had begun while I finished an accelerated real estate course. Construction began on the east side of the typical two-story concrete motel, as the transformation began to take place. I was rather surprised and educated in a new trend to which the vacationing public was headed—time share, which I could not understand. The other half of the motel continued to operate and generate revenue. The sales force of hot shots was another matter. I know why Mr. Ahern asked me to be the general manager of this operation—to be the peacekeeper. The salespeople were quite a collection of characters that would tell the "Ups" (guest/customers) anything to sell a unit (one week). Even though I had some hustle in me, I knew immediately that I could not con the nice people to buy while they were enjoying their vacation. Our salespeople would get a hold of a nice couple from Iowa and would hammer them into signing a purchase contract—even with the down payment on their credit card! They gave them a gift or tickets to Disney World and invited them to the general manager's cocktail party.

The salespeople were neatly dressed, smooth talking with a big smile and a great line of bull. A car salesman didn't have anything on these guys and dolls. The ironic thing about these characters was that they were likable and fun to be around. As soon as they finished their shifts they would be in the bar spending their spiffs (daily incentives). Even as hard as I was on them, they would always buy me a drink. The boiler room gang was a fun bunch.

The architect and designer were on schedule in stripping two rooms and transforming them into one spacious, well-appointed suite. As time passed, I understood why Mr. Ahern converted a successful two-story, well-located motel into a time share resort. Simple mathematics: 100 units x 52 units (weeks) x $4,000 = $20,800,000 vs. $4,000,000 worth of real estate. Plus—open-end, maintenance-fee! Wow! This appeared to be a new trend in the hospitality industry. Several other developers throughout the Disney area began new time share projects. The area became a rat race with offsite spots. OPCs (off-property contractors) were set up at gas stations, gift shops, hotel lobbies, convenience stores. They would offer gifts and free attraction tickets to take a tour (hard-sell presentation). Eventually, time share would be called interim ownership, vacation clubs, vacation ownership, or any other marketable term that could be sold to the traveling public. All was going well, as Jo-Jo and I were buying some properties near Disney World and in Cocoa Beach, knowing that at the end of any commitment to Mr. Ahern I would be out of a job again. I began to set up my own management company. Since working for management companies, I had discovered any hotel's management was only as good as the on-site manager. I would create a small company and manage the properties myself.

At the end of the year, the motel had been totally renovated and was known as The Magic Tree Resort. It was a beautiful little property with its new exciting decor in its bright colors and its exotic tropical landscaping. Sales were at a very brisk pace, ownership was happy, and I was bored. Mr. Ahern rewarded me with a lucrative bonus and wanted me to continue to manage the resort. I thanked him and told him that I was a hotel man, not a time-share person. My heart was not in the business.

In the meantime, I had met several foreign developers—one from England, two from India, one from Lebanon, and one from California. What a mixture of personalities. I had lunch with Mr. Lewis Cartier from London, who was redeveloping a property known as Little England. As he began to lay out his plans, I thought this would be a major project—600 acres, a 600-room resort hotel, 27-hole championship golf course, an English village with restaurants, shops, and pubs, and 250 condominiums. He informed me that he reduced the size of the original development and that he released an experienced former Disney staff. As I reviewed the detailed model, I thought it was a very special and exciting project. How do I determine a fee providing Mr. Cartier makes me an offer? Mr. Cartier was an extremely hardworking little Englishman who was a self-made multimillionaire. We immediately showed mutual respect for one another. When I left, I felt very confident and positive even though Mr.

Cartier was interviewing other people over the next three days.

The following evening as I was preparing another proposal, Mr. Cartier called and offered me an astonishing contract. It was twice the amount of the fee that I had in mind as well as a condo in the future. I tried to play it cool but I was elated with the deal. I met Mr. Cartier at his office the next day and finished the contract. I agreed to begin work the next day. When I left his office, I thought I was still dreaming. Excitedly, I drove home to tell Jo-Jo and celebrate with her.

For the next nine months we would work from 8:00 A.M. until 7:00–8:00 P.M. Mr. Cartier, Howard (construction project manager), Valerie (administrative assistant), and I put all our hearts and souls into the project. Our enthusiasm and dedication was steadfast and loyal. The village was 80 percent complete. The second floor was being constructed on the hotel while the golf course was beginning to take shape. I had begun to hire staff and had finished the marketing plan.

Mr. Cartier would fly back and forth to England via the Concorde on a regular basis. Early one Monday morning, Mr. Cartier called me into his office to inform me that he was selling the property. He said that he was going back to England with his new wife and family. He asked me to inform the staff. Since I was in complete shock, I had to take a walk before meeting with the staff. I called a luncheon staff meeting to advise everyone of the very sad news. Being professionals, all took the news well. Mr. Cartier paid everyone six weeks' severance pay. Mr. Cartier was a true gentleman and honored my contract with full payment. I told the staff that I was buying cocktails after work. Everyone joined me to drown their sorrows. This was the hardest and saddest situation that I had to present to Jo-Jo. My dream had been totally crushed!

We went to the beach to relax and finish four proposals that I had begun working on a few months previously. In a couple of days, reality set in and I got back to work. Within two weeks, I drafted five proposals. Within four weeks, I heard from three developers. I accepted two contracts and rejected another.

The first project to come out of the ground was the Brock Residence Inn. This was the first all-suite hotel in Orlando. The buildings were constructed like townhouses and were spread over five acres. It was a great facility for the guests but an operational nightmare for the housekeeping and maintenance staff. This was the ultimate example of "the more you give the public, the more they want."

The suites provided all the basic guest supplies as well as shampoo, conditioner, full kitchen, coffee maker, coffee supplies, popcorn maker/popcorn, free breakfast, and even complimentary cocktails—too much! We could not keep suite attendants (housekeepers) because of the extra work and responsibilities. I finally created an incentive program to establish better pay for better help. The labor market was drying up because of two reasons: too much hotel development and the Disney empire. "A suite for the price of a room" sold the public. Business was good at the Residence Inn and good for me as I picked up another contract.

After the first year of operations, dealing with the owner became extremely difficult. I intended to finish my commitment to Sam, but he and I engaged in verbal combat that led to an ugly situation. I had always maintained my composure but with his sharp insults and his questioning my ability, I lost it. I threw the hotel keys and suggested that he "stick his hotel where the sun doesn't shine." The egotistical Samuel Hartford, owner, not only hit on our sales representative, Kim, but he was extremely critical and demanding. I had mailed a certified letter with a written ninety-day termination notice per our agreement. I had began developing a business plan for the Golden Towers Travelodge in Kissimmee.

Without knowledge of what was to come, I had entered into a contract with a Middle Eastern developer who came to the United States through Canada. After leaving the property, I went to Bennigan's and called Omar Ahamad, the developer of the Travelodge. He asked me to meet him at the Marriott's lounge. I researched his mysterious background and discovered that he built three small motels on the 192 strip and owned a six-thousand-square-foot home in Arnold Palmer's Bay Meadows. He drove a new Mercedes Benz sedan and knew all the cocktail waitresses at the Marriott. He also lived with a very classy, educated little lady that was his silent partner. Omar was a husky, rather handsome middle-aged man who had a broad smile with a smooth line. From all appearances, Omar looked like the real deal. I should have remembered what Bob told me, "It takes three Jews to stay up with one Lebanese."

As the construction of the two-hundred-room lakefront hotel was nearing completion, I presented Omar with a business plan. He got excited about the plans for his hotel, and we finished our agreement within two hours. It was my standard eighteen pages of babble. I thought that after a very expensive legal fee, I would be protected under the conditions of the contract. Anyway, with my usual eager enthusiasm I attacked the project with all my strength. It took me a while to realize that business was a dog-eat-dog world. I hired the sales manager, Kim, from the Residence Inn, Kathy as front-office manager and Hank, the bar manager, from The Magic Tree Resort. I also hired some of my former housekeepers. I was very fortunate to assemble a professional staff in the tough labor market. While Kim and I became very aggressive in marketing and sales, Omar was preparing the property for our grand opening. Nearing the opening, I asked Omar when the swimming pool would be complete. He replied (his first lie), "I am having problems with the contractor." The truth came out a few days later while Omar was in Canada trying to raise money—the contractor had not been paid.

My staff and I opened the beautiful pyramid-style hotel on a shoestring. No grand opening, no marketing funds, and very little operating capital created a no-win situation. Omar thought with a good location and an experienced staff he would be rolling in the dough. He forgot that being undercapitalized was the primary reason that any business fails. I had to pay the pool contractor from operating funds.

While we struggled with the hotel the first year, I continued to search for other contracts. I was forced to seek other revenue since Omar failed to pay six months of my contracted fees. He agreed to lease me the cocktail lounge in lieu of my fees. Times were tough again in the Orlando market with another overbuilt condition.

Through one of my peers, I heard about some pending troubled properties. I requested and was granted a conference with Judge Cecil Brown, who was overseeing these cases. During our meeting Judge Brown with his heavy Southern accent asked, "Why do you think that you can manage these properties for the court better than anyone else?"

I answered, "Simple, your Honor, that's what I do for a living. I'm not a CPA, banker, or an attorney."

He smiled and said, "Mr. Wayne, with that answer and your resumé I would like to appoint you the receiver of the Vienna Motel." I gratefully thanked the stereotypical senior Southern judge. He had the reputation of being firm, honest, and just. The judge's assistant passed along the files on the property to me. I excitedly left the judge's chambers and headed to the little motel.

As I approached the inn, I gave it my usual curb-appeal review. It was a cute little twenty-eight-unit motel that had a quaint European appearance. The German owners had left and had gone back to Germany. The nice little lady on the desk was in charge, so I presented the court order. Susan was very cooperative as I reviewed the situation and plans. I called Jo-Jo to advise her of the outcome of the meeting with the judge. Jo laughed and asked, "Who is going to manage the inn?"

I humbly asked, "Would you be interested in being the innkeeper for a nice little inn?" Of course, she said yes, as always. That was a relief because for my first receivership,

I had to have someone who was honest and a detailed perfectionist.

Even though Omar owed me six figures in fees and incentives, I held on because of my loyal staff, and I had given my word. With continued lies to me and my staff along with bounced payroll checks, the stress was overwhelming. Omar could never recover because of being undercapitalized in the beginning. Without my knowledge, Omar and his lawyer were scheming to file Chapter 11, and one day I read in the newspaper that they had done just that. My attorney and I filed for judgment in trying to collect some of my fees. We had our hearing with Federal Judge Proctor, who granted Omar's voluntary bankruptcy (Chapter 11). Instead of justice being served, the judge declared that Omar could continue operating the hotel as long as he filed a plan for recovery. All creditors (including my company) could not pursue collecting their debts, and Judge Proctor declared my lease on the lounge was null and void! I objected and was found in contempt of court. In the minds of federal judges, they think of themselves as gods! How does our justice system work? A foreigner (not paying taxes) brings relatives into the country illegally, files bankruptcy, does not pay his bills, continues to operate his hotel, takes my booming cocktail lounge, owes me one and a half years of labor while continuing to live in a million-dollar home. It didn't figure. For whom were the laws of the country written? Not its citizens or victims!

Meanwhile, Judge Brown—what a difference in gods—gave me three more receiverships. He called me within two months to oversee a motel, a campground, and two hundred mini-warehouses. All was well, with the exception of not knowing what to charge for my services and sending the judge too many reports.

Disney World continued to expand and add theme parks, and they were building hotel rooms as were other developers. Sea World expanded and Universal Studios had opened. Central Florida had begun to boom again, and I was on a roll again. I continued to operate as a receiver until the Honorable Judge Brown retired. During this time I also operated the Hilton Gateway Hotel and the Radisson Lake Buena Vista. Most owners have never managed a hotel, but they knew how to demand a healthy bottom line.

As the general public became more and more impatient, the hotels continued to try to streamline with express check-in and check-out. While managing the Lake Buena Vista Radisson Hotel, we installed an express check-out system. This simply meant that the night auditor posted all charges, posted the lazy guest's credit card, checked him or her out, and put the receipt under the guest's door. The guest did not have to check out at the front desk. One evening, my senior night auditor (Lisa) was delivering these bills/receipts at approximately 2:30 A.M. when she spotted a beautiful, drunk, naked woman in the hall. Lisa knocked on the door by where the lady was standing, told her that she could not be in the hall and please stay in her room. A tall, dark, and handsome gentleman opened the door with a rather astonished look upon his face. Lisa continued as she helped the hapless lady into the room, "Sir, you must keep your wife in the room."

The middle-aged man with a broad, boyish smile said, "I . . . uh . . . have never seen this lady . . . uh . . . until now—

but thanks." Lisa just about died with embarrassment, turned a bright red, and asked the smiling guest if she could borrow a robe. While questioning the blonde, she could not remember the room number but insisted it was the correct floor. Lisa knocked on the door across the hall. Bingo! A drunken man opened the door and asked his wife, "What's the matter, Honey, you couldn't sleep, got lost, and who's your friend?" Lisa shoved the woman into the room and ran back to the front desk.

In real life, I have been stuck in elevators, but like you see in the movies, I had never been stuck with a pregnant lady. A few weeks later on a normal quiet Wednesday afternoon, I was coming down in one of the elevators when it stopped between the third and fourth floors. In the car with me were a young pregnant girl, her friend, a little boy, and a man in his late thirties. I tried to reassure everyone that the car would be moving soon. I rang the alarm and called the front desk. A few minutes elapsed, and of course the lady expecting began to complain about pains (oh, please, not labor ones). Her friend began to get loud and abusive. The feminine man began to sweat and prance while the little boy thought it was an adventure. After fifteen minutes I called the desk to check on the situation—maintenance man off property, elevator company called and on the way. I told the front-desk clerk to call for an ambulance. I knew I had to take action. I had the young girl and the young man lock their arms while they braced themselves against the side of the car. With a small running start I vaulted to catch a hold on the escape hatch located on top of the car. For some unknown reason, I had the extra strength to force the hatch open. I struggled to pull myself through the hole and on top of the greasy car. As I stood upright I could hear the expectant lady saying the pains were getting closer. Again, as I reached the doors of the next floor, I found extra adrenaline and was able to force the doors open. I ran downstairs to the maintenance shop and found the wrench/key to open the doors of the stuck car. I pried open the door, and all was well except the future mother. First, I pulled out the little boy and told the girl and man to help push the mother to me. Carefully, I pulled her out and put her on a rollaway. The others safely followed. The ambulance arrived and a bouncing baby boy was born on the way to the hospital. Mother and baby Chance did fine.

While at the Hilton Gateway, I oversaw a million-dollar renovation that went smoothly as we maintained an occupancy in the high eighties. The most difficult task as the GM was to maintain a full staff for the 350-unit hotel with its restaurants, bars, and convention center. As the line from the movies goes, "Build it and they will come." The greater Orlando/Kissimmee area had built more hotel rooms than any other city in the world! That included New York City, Chicago, Los Angeles, London, Paris, and Tokyo.

The hotel ran quite efficiently without too many incidents. On occasion I would have to discipline an employee and cater to a guest's every wish. On a warm Friday evening Michele, a new front-desk clerk, double rented a room. Michele handed the room key to Jerry, a new bellman, and he proceeded to show the guest to the room. Without knocking (every hotel employee should *always* knock), Jerry entered the room. Upon his surprise, a couple was seriously making love! The red-faced bellman apologized and backed out of the room. Of course, the other guest wanted to know what was going on. Jerry took the guest directly back to the front desk and reassigned another room to the new guest. Of course, in a few moments the disturbed guests called for the manager. Again, because of the employee's errors I had to beg apologies, buy two dinners, and give away a free room! I headed to our new lounge for a cocktail and to listen to my friends Mark and Lorna Wayne.

The next morning, I wrote another memo concerning security. It highlighted the issuing of room keys, giving out room numbers over the phone or over the front desk, and the basic practice of knocking on all room doors twice before entering the door!

Just a few years ago, Orlando was a beautiful, quiet, sophisticated, small city while Kissimmee was a small, friendly "cowboy" town with one main street. Both small communities were surrounded by chains of picturesque lakes, rolling orange groves, massive cattle ranches, and an occasional alligator. When the Disney Corporation began to develop, it turned the lovely central Florida area upside down—good or bad?

Not only did the hotels suffer for labor, all the service and retail outlets needed help. Even as Orlando grew at a tremendous rate, the unemployment rate remained at zero. The quality of workers continued to show in our society in the quality of service performed. Generally, though, pride in a good day's work continued to decrease throughout the industry in guest satisfaction. The area boomed too fast. On that subject, I stayed upset with Disney, local politics, and greedy owners. I organized a new commerce association, and became an outspoken officer in the hotel/motel association, as well as the fifth investor in Osceola Park (a new horse track) within ten miles of the "Mouse House." I thought if the venture was good enough for the local good old boys, powerful ranchers, and investors such as Mike Wallace, then it should be a solid venture, and maybe someday the horses would be running.

Disney World, the hustlers, the traffic, the T-shirt shops (owned by foreigners that couldn't speak English), the politics, and the tourists finally drove me to the breaking point. Time to move on!

CHAPTER 7

TENNESSEE

1987

At an association meeting, I had met an East Indian gentleman who indicated that he needed help with his hotels. I finished my obligations in Kissimmee and I met with Amir Zamadi. We drafted a contract for management of his eight hotels in the Volunteer State. We set up a central office in Nashville to operate hotels in Nashville, Memphis, Chattanooga, Cookeville, Manchester, and Murphysboro. This appeared to be another exciting and interesting challenge. Jo-Jo would handle the sales and marketing while I would handle operations. We visited each property—Days Inns and Travelodges—to analyze their condition, staff, and atmosphere. Each property was different and had its own personality as did each city.

Nashville was famous for being country, but it was very cosmopolitan with its varied industries, the music industry, Vanderbilt University, Opryland, and the magnificent Opryland Hotel.

The Days Inn properties in Nashville needed major capital renovation and a good deep cleaning. The inns in the smaller cities were in better condition and operated by female managers. The two properties in Memphis were opposite of each other—The Days Inn in town was in fair condition, neat, and clean. The Airport Travelodge needed improvements, a good cleaning, and a new manager. I replaced three managers, wrote a business and marketing plan, and set up a manager's meeting.

While I concentrated on cleaning up the properties and putting them in order, Jo-Jo concentrated on marketing the very difficult Inns. This was a challenge because Amir had not put any capital into the properties. As I would get one property under control, I would hear a panic call from another inn. I had vice squad officers contact me about two properties: one concerning the Nashville Days Inn about prostitution and the other in Memphis about drugs at the Travelodge. I made appointments with two officers. They both wanted to set up "stings" at the motels. I agreed because the reputations of the inns were as bad as the Motel 6.

Sgt. J.D. Avery informed me that a group of ladies of the evening were moving around the area between three or four motels. He explained that the pimp would rent the room for three or four days while the "girls" would work different shifts from the streets. Some would work in pairs while training a new "young lady." J.D. set up a room next door to the "John" room. The girls would do the John in a short time and have the John drop them back on the streets. Not only did the police film the girls but they filmed the John's tag and automobile. Then J.D. sent his undercover squad into action. Within twenty-four hours, the squad had arrested nine hookers. One young girl (sixteen years old) broke down and led J.D. to her pimp. "Pump Daddy," as he called himself, was Tyrone Davis, who had a rap sheet as long as a frog's tongue. I was very happy to see that J.D.

would break a regulation in the name of justice. He personally put Gloria Lou Smith, the young hooker, on the Greyhound Bus and sent her back home to her parents at the farm. After that, the word spread, and we did not see any more working girls around the Days Inn on Murphysboro Road.

A week later, I met Lt. Allen Thomas and Sgt. Clyde Washington at their Memphis office to review their plans for the sting at the Travelodge. Each day of my life, I continued to learn something new. Allen, Clyde, and I went to the inn to set up their rooms. When I showed the officers the designated rooms, they began to show me where the drug pushers and users would hide their stash. Not only the obvious spots—behind pictures, mirrors, furniture, under and inside mattresses, box springs, and pillows—Allen picked up the lamp, flipped it over, and took off the base while Clyde took off the back of the TV set. They continued through the room by taking the room apart—the toilet tank, the air conditioner unit, the smoke alarm, base boards, backs and bases of the furniture, and even the electrical outlets. I was amazed how the twisted criminal mind works.

The following weekend, Allen sent in his shoddy-looking undercover agents. The same slick usual suspects checked in to set up their business. This procedure had become a regular occurrence. When the same characters checked in, they began to receive numerous local telephone calls. By Sunday morning, four drug traffickers had been taken away in handcuffs. As I left the property, I felt proud that I had a small involvement in busting such lowlifes. I also felt better leaving because I had hired Tom Morgan, a mature, strong, experienced hotel man as the general manager.

On a quiet Saturday afternoon at the Park Place Days Inn, I was training a new room clerk. I felt that Kim could handle the desk while I went to have a late lunch. By the time I returned, I had several guest complaints about noise from a room. I asked Kim what happened while I was gone. She said a gentleman came in and asked for a key to his wife's room. I asked if she requested any identification. With a blank, dumb look on her face, she said, "No, sir." I called the room in question with no answer. I told Kim to call the police while I headed toward the noisy room. As I was walking down the hallway, I heard a gun shot. I ran toward the sound. Before I reached the room, I saw a man with a gun in his hand run out of the room. He headed toward the exit to the parking lot and sped off in his pick-up. When I arrived at the room, a hysterical woman in her mid-forties was bent over a young man in his twenties. They were half clad. The young man had been shot but apparently not seriously. The police arrived and took charge. The young man was sent to the hospital, and the assailant was apprehended within the hour. Final story—the woman was having an affair with her nephew (by marriage) and they were caught by the husband/uncle. All room clerks must be discreet and never hand out keys without guest approval or ID identification!

We continued to clean up the properties without the help of the owner—no capital improvements. Jo-Jo had booked several bus operators for some of the inns. The managers and I had recruited the best people available. All was going as well as possible given the conditions of the properties. My stress level reached its highest point—a high blood pressure pill daily!

I would constantly receive panic calls from one of the managers. Sam Marshall called from the other Days Inn in Nashville. He began telling me about a sweet older farm couple, Hershel and Mary Campbell, that stayed with him every time they came to town. Sam went on to tell me that Mary had passed away and that Hershel was drunk and very upset when he checked in. Sam said that he was very worried about Mr. Campbell because Heather, the front desk clerk, thought she saw a gun stuck in his trousers. I jumped in my automobile and raced across town to the Inn. I called Mr. Campbell's room and no one answered. Before calling the police, I thought that we should check the room. Sam and I knocked loudly and said, "Management." I repeated the knock even louder with no answer. As Sam and I entered the room, a pitiful Mr. Campbell was sitting at the table staring into space with a bottle of Jack Daniels in one hand and a .38 revolver in the other. As I approached Hershel, he lifted the gun to his head. I stopped quietly and softly said, "Hershel, Mary is looking down upon you and is very upset with you right now. She asked me to tell you 'to put down the gun because if you kill yourself you will not be with her in heaven.'" He hesitated, laid the pistol on the table, and began to cry. I immediately went to him and hugged him. Meanwhile Sam had left to call the police. They came on the property with sirens blasting and lights flashing, as did the paramedics. Mr. Campbell and I walked out of the room as the officers rushed up to us. I stepped in front of Mr. Campbell and told the officer in charge of the situation to be gentle because he needed help, not jail. I continued by explaining the circumstances.

One week later, Tom called me from the Memphis Travelodge and said there had been a murder. I flew to the property to find out the details. Tom informed me that a young, beautiful black girl had been raped and her body thrown off the third floor. I reviewed the incident report and called the investigating officer. He told me that the young lady was babysitting for one of our guests and she appeared to know her assailant. The fifteen-year-old was raped and murdered in the room, then thrown over the railing. The police department had questioned the staff even though the gruesome act had been committed around one o'clock in the morning, which meant that the night auditor and the security guard were the only staff on duty. I asked Howard, the night auditor, if he heard anything. He said that the whole night was quiet until Leroy, the security guard, came and reported the girl's body. Howard said he immediately called 911.

The next morning, I met with Lieutenant Johnson, the investigator. He said the whole situation was very strange. He questioned the family, the girl's friends, and the hotel staff. He continued by saying that they had taken Leroy into custody. He said something wasn't right with him because he was too calm and casual. Leroy had worked for the security company for over six months and was always well mannered and polite. The owner of the security company informed us that Leroy had recently been honorably discharged from the U.S. Army.

Three days later Leroy broke and admitted to the horrible crime. He said the young girl had been flirting with him all evening and invited him inside the room. He said, "Things got out of hand." She began to scream and he panicked. Leroy said he tried to silence her but instead he suffocated the girl. He thought—if he threw her over the railing, the authorities would think it was an accident because he reported it to the front desk. What a senseless act and a waste of two lives as well as the hurt of others.

A few months later, Leroy got life in prison with no possibility of parole. I received a notice for suit from the family of the dead girl. What was ironic about the whole situation was—Leroy worked for a prominent outside security agency sworn to protect our guests. Before the child's body was cold, the divorced mother was after some cash! What a crazy world!

After these intense experiences, I would take advantage of the perks and opportunities while in Memphis. I would visit Beale Street to enjoy the blues joints. One evening I had the opportunity to see Jerry Lee and B.B. King—the same night! While in Nashville, I would trade out rooms for tickets to see popular entertainers at the Starwood Amphitheater—Jimmy Buffet, Hank Williams Jr., Kenny Rogers, Dolly, and others. Even with this, the variety of parks in the beautiful mountains, particularly in the fall, was the highlight of the state.

The managers, Jo-Jo, and I had done all we could with the properties, even with the lack of capital funds. The last straw with Mr. Zamadi was when payroll checks began to bounce and his secretary told me that he was in Canada. I immediately went to the bank and deposited five thousand dollars (personal money) to cover the employees' checks. Amir finally returned my call three days later. I decided to terminate our agreement, and I gave Amir thirty days' notice. He would not accept my notice, but I insisted and sent a certified written notice. Jo-Jo and Mark flew back to Florida while I began to complete my obligations. On the thirtieth day, no one showed up from the Orlando corporate office. I called Sam, my senior manager, to my office. I met with Sam and Debbie, my administrative assistant, to review what was pending with each property, including bus tour arrivals.

I visited each hotel, thanked everyone, and said my farewells. After three years, we gave it our best but I could not handle the stress. As I left the great state of Tennessee, I looked back at its beauty and the warmth of its people. I had completed each year's contract with confidence and pride. Back to Florida to seek out new contracts.

CHAPTER 8
CENTRAL FLORIDA
1990

Again, another short beach vacation and back to the Kissimmee/Orlando area. My good friend Thomas Grant had called and informed me that a new trend had developed. Small individual investors were buying vacation homes to rent. Since Tom knew that I had continued to keep my real estate license active, he introduced me to two aggressive builders. Each contractor was building homes and townhouses. They were selling them before they were completed. The majority of the buyers were from the United Kingdom, and they needed management. The British planned to use their units four to eight weeks annually and wanted them rented the balance of the year. I felt the homes and townhouses could be marketed and managed just as hotels—maybe easier. Through the introduction by the builders to the investors, I began to build a great variety of units in my portfolio. The sale prices of the units ranged from $75,000 to $350,000.

Within a few months, I had signed over one hundred individual management contracts. I had begun to advertise nationally, creating a demand for "a vacation home for the price of a hotel room." Actually, managing homes proved to be easier than managing hotels because of less staff and not being open 365 days a year, 24 hours per day! Dealing with a few owners proved to be very difficult at times. Those particular owners thought that I should rent their units first and they should be 100 percent occupied. Wrong! I rotated rental requests in order by special needs.

As I continued to build my management company, my reputation grew throughout the community. I acquired a contract for a two-hundred-unit Quality Inn in Kissimmee as well as another court-appointed receivership. I was back into the tourist business again. I loved and appreciated them, but I would like to mention a few drawbacks for this particular trade.

Most common questions:

What is your cheapest room?
What discounts do you offer?
Do you have free transportation to the attractions?
Do you give a free breakfast?
What's your single rate? (six people waiting in the station wagon)
Can I have eight towels for the pool?
Do you have an iron and a hair dryer? (not always returned)

Most common guest practices:

Trashed rooms with items missing.
Pockets and bags stuffed from the buffet.

Parking lots used as a dumpster! (People just dump trash and cigarette ashtrays by their vehicles, then drive away to a gas station that has trash receptacles by the gas pumps. Why?)

Items reported missing from room, and guests blame the housekeeper for theft. Then they go home and claim their losses against their homeowner's insurance policy. Usually, they left the items at home or never lost them at all. All hotels have safes and/or safety deposit boxes.

Guests slip and fall by the pool while running and want to sue the hotel.

God love 'em, though. They paid the bills!

I just loved the Yankee snowbirds that flooded to Florida in the winter season. One cool evening (72 degrees) at the Quality Inn, Mrs. Hoover from Iowa called the front desk. In her hysterical voice said, "Listen, someone needs to come to my room immediately!"

Tommy, my cool and humorous room clerk, asked, "Ma'am, what is the problem?"

She exclaimed, "There is a giant ugly bug in my room!"

Tommy was a Florida "cracker" (born and raised in Florida) with a weird sense of humor and enjoyed messing with people's minds. He asked, "Ma'am, calm down and give me a description of the critter."

She began by saying, "It's about three to four inches long, an inch wide, black in color with wings and a big head."

Tommy, with a cheeky smile, continued by asking, "Is it dead or alive?"

Mrs. Hoover answered, "I don't know."

Tommy, holding back his laughter, instructed the guest by asking, "Do you have an umbrella or a long object to check the condition of the animal?"

She answered, "Yes, sir, I do have an umbrella."

Tommy, about to wet his pants at this point, said, "Ma'am, would you touch the bug to determine its condition?"

She sheepishly agreed. As Mrs. Hoover touched the insect, Tommy heard her scream with relief. She got back on the telephone and informed Tommy that the vermin was deceased.

Tommy continued by saying, "Mrs. Hoover, thanks for being so brave. That type of bug is known as a Palmetto bug and won't hurt you, but they release a terrible odor. I will have maintenance come and remove your new friend." I had walked up and caught the gist of what was happening. Tommy had not seen me, but Cathy, the other room clerk, continued laughing while pointing at me. Tommy was still cracking up when he noticed me. As his face became flushed, I smiled and walked away as Tommy began, "Boss, I didn't. . . ."

I interrupted and said, "Don't bother."

As all hotels do, I would run a classified advertisement for help on a regular basis. The hospitality industry personnel grew worse each year. It appeared that the new "breed" of employees lacked pride and respect for their jobs. Every excuse would come first and before their jobs—"I've got to go to my husband's fourth cousin's funeral." "It's my third month's anniversary with my new boyfriend. I didn't have gas but I saw his car at the local pub." "My baby cried all night, so now I need to sleep." The best one—Clyde, my assistant maintenance man's grandmother died three times the same year!

As I interviewed new applicants, I would ask, "Why do you want to work in the hotel business?" Seventy-five percent of them would say, "Oh, I love to work with the public," or "I love people." Two weeks later, they would be saying, "What a bitch. I can't stand this or that!" The employees who complained the most were always the laziest. Oh well, at that point I would look at each and every individual as an asset. Good traits (credits) versus bad habits (debits) and if the credits would show at the bottom line, they would stay.

Thank goodness for Jo-Jo, Mark, and my dad as they helped me manage and maintain the homes. I continued to pursue more hotel management contracts. During this time, I had the pleasure of seeing Harris Rosen again. Harris had become the largest independent hotel owner in the Orlando market. I always knew that he would do well.

Within six months, I had acquired agreements to assume management of three other properties. Again, I was on a roll. First I took control of the Riverfront Hotel in Melbourne, Florida, owned by an East Indian gentleman. The next property was a Rodeway Inn near Kennedy Space Center owned by an eccentric Dutchman. The third property, a Ramada Inn located in South Florida, was owned by a Hispanic group. At this point in my career, I felt as if I was working for the United Nations.

In the fall of 1992, Jo-Jo called me to meet her and one of our British clients in Kissimmee. I met them at the popular Fox and Hound Pub. As we enjoyed a few pints, John Sheffield asked, "Chance, do you know of a business that I could purchase?"

I said, "John, everything in America is for sale. I need to know what type and how much you want to invest?"

He continued by saying, "My wild son has fallen in love with a damn Yank, nothing personal."

"Nothing taken, since I fell in love with a beautiful damn Limey," I replied, laughing. We all laughed and ordered another round of drinks.

Jokingly, I said, "John, you own property here and in the U.K. You are astute in the business of property management. I'll sell you my business."

John looked directly into my glassy eyes and asked how much.

I said, "One hundred thousand dollars."

He smiled, ordered another round, and said, "Deal." He continued by saying, "With one condition—you teach my son the business."

We shook hands and I said, "Deal." Jo-Jo excused herself to go home, as John and I continued to have "just one more." We both wrote down the particulars on cocktail napkins as John insisted on a close immediately. We signed the closing documents within a week, and my staff and I began training John Jr. I only sold the management contracts for the homes and townhouses while I maintained the management of the hotels. This relieved me of one major portion of my stressful life. The Sheffields were a class act; they paid cash and learned the business in a fast and efficient manner. The last I heard, they continued operating the business very successfully, and young John had married his love.

Meanwhile, on the east coast of Florida my challenges continued with the owners, guests, and particularly the employees. My resident manager, Thomas, at the Riverfront Hotel called me to report an accident at the property. Thomas was a young, naïve, Christian man who was very conscientious and gullible. The older, seasoned maintenance man, Harry, claimed that he severely injured his back while moving an air conditioner unit. This was ironic since Harry was extremely lazy and always had his assistants move any heavy items. Thomas had excused Harry for the day and advised him to seek medical attention. When I was away from the property, Harry showed contempt toward Thomas and would simply disappear at times. Since he had been at the property for several years, he felt he ran the hotel.

When I arrived at the hotel, Thomas had completed an incident report and had begun to fill out the state-required forms for all worker's compensation claims. This report had to be filed with the state and the insurance carrier within seventy-two hours. Thomas and I reviewed the incident and questioned the other members of the staff. Even though Harry was not well liked by his fellow employees, they all denied witnessing the accident. Since there were rumors that the hotel was being sold and we had no benefits, we had doubt that Harry had a legitimate injury. I finished reviewing the operation with Thomas and told him to keep me informed about Harry. I went into his employee file to find out his address for future observation.

I called Jo-Jo and told her to pack for a long weekend in Jamaica. She asked, "When did this come about?" I said about an hour ago. I told Jo that we needed a break and some time together. I told her that I traded out (bartered) the vacation. We left Thursday night from West Palm and arrived at the island in a couple of hours. I should have remembered how the island moved—slow. It took as long to pass customs and rent a car as long as it took to fly. After receiving the dirty, untidy automobile we stopped for fuel (car was empty). Before I could get out of the vehicle, a hustler was by my side trying to peddle dope, women, or anything. I ran him off! Driving to the island resort was another experience—people all over the road, animals in the road, and the roads full of holes. When we arrived at the resort, the hospitality was good with our suite adequately clean.

The next day we went sailing on the Raging Lady Schooner with Captain Blood at the wheel. He gave us the thrilling, wet cruise of a lifetime. Later that evening the captain and his lady met us for drinks at the hotel. He entertained us with his tales about his celebrity clientele.

We had a sensational, fun, lovemaking three days until rushing back to the airport. The local policemen had set up a speed trap on the primary highway. I was traveling six miles above the speed limit (forty-one miles per hour). They treated me as if I was Dillinger. I was hurried behind the head man's car. Since I travel with credit cards, I only had $128. He settled on that amount as my fine and released me. Jo-Jo and I were happy to land back in the good old USA!

I headed back to South Florida to check on the Ramada Resort while Jo-Jo worked with the Sheffields and oversaw the warehouses (another court receivership). The Ramada was a two-hundred-unit full-service property in the beach area. Every time I approached the property, I regretted not learning to speak fluent Spanish. Seventy-five percent of the staff could not speak or write English. I had hired a Spanish-American general manager who was very strict but understanding. He ran a very tight ship. I needed a strong manager in that labor market and part of Florida.

Being in South Florida, our season was in the winter—catering to the snowbirds. In the off-season, we could complete our maintenance projects and capital improvements. The Latin ownership was a rather fiery group of individuals. It appeared that they could not agree on anything. As the management company, I would often get in the middle and remind them that we had one objective—to make money. I would then have to remind them how to accomplish that in the hotel business. None of the investors had ever been in the hospitality business. The manager, Victor, always showed loyalty and support toward me. He would call me when one of the owners arrived on property and began to get involved in the operation. Because the Hispanic community was close by nature, hiring relatives were common and expected. Victor tried not to follow the expected but rather enforce our company policies. After inspecting the inn and reviewing the operation with Victor, we had dinner and I headed north on Interstate 95. As I drove the very congested highway, I had a very strange and eerie feeling come over me. I felt it had something to do with the Ramada.

Jo-Jo and I met at home in Cocoa Beach to review our business and spend a weekend together. We finally enjoyed a quiet two days at the beach without any panic calls from the properties. I did receive a call from Professor Winston of Brevard Community College. He taught business and hospitality courses at the school. He asked me to be a guest speaker for his hospitality management class with the subject being "The Labor Market and Opportunities in the Industry." I agreed even though I only had three days to prepare. I knew how to paint a beautiful picture of the industry, but I needed to stress the importance of dedication, long hours, and commitment for success in the business. As I researched facts and figures for the class, I discovered a simple fact for myself. There are 168 hours in the week and if someone worked only 40 hours per week, that is only 23.8 percent of one's time for their livelihood!

Monday morning came quick, and I went to the Rodeway Inn to meet with the owner. The Dutchman was strong in marketing and was away from the property a great deal. He had done a good job with an older property. He was very active in the community and was wired into the local politicians. When he was away, I would oversee the Inn. Mr. Van Hausen was a big, strapping man in his early sixties. He was very frugal, demanding, and at times rather rude. When he was in town, he was a hands-on owner/manager. When he was away, the staff had a sigh of relief.

One Thursday evening when Mr. Van Hausen was in Europe, one of his so-called friends stopped by the hotel. That evening, we were two rooms short of selling out. He identified himself as Roger Downing, county commissioner and a personal friend of the Dutchman. He told Robert, the room clerk, that Mr. Van Hausen always "comped" his room (gave it to him for free). While Mr. Downing was intimidating Robert, I walked out of my office and asked, "What's the problem, may I help?"

He inquired, "Who are you and can we reach the owner?"

I snapped, "I am the general manager, and the owner is out of the country!"

Mr. Downing had become belligerent due to much liquor and was being downright rude to Robert and me. He demanded that he was going to get a free room. I insisted that he wasn't getting *any* room! He reached across the front desk and I pushed his hand away. I told Mr. Downing to leave the property and for Robert to call the police.

Downing shouted, "I'll have your job!"

I slammed the hotel keys down on the front desk and said, "You can have it—then I won't have to put up with arrogant bastards like you!" He staggered out the door, got in his automobile (where a young woman was waiting), and spun off in a hurry.

Robert stared at me and said, "Boss, I have never seen you so angry. I don't ever want you mad at me."

I apologized to Robert as the police arrived. I knew Jim Henderson, the officer that answered the call. I described the incident, gave a description of the commissioner's vehicle, and pointed in the direction in which he headed. Jim said, "Thanks, Chance, I would love to bust a county commissioner for a D.W.I."

I said, "Call me if you catch him." Jim smiled and said that he would.

I met my buddies, Irish Joe, Wild Jerry, and The Houseman in the lounge for a cocktail. About an hour later, I received a telephone call from Officer Henderson. He reported that he had busted the commissioner for driving while under the influence. Jim continued by saying that "Mr. Hot Shot" resisted arrest, and that he had to call for back up. He laughed and said, "We had to take him to jail in handcuffs."

When Van Hausen returned from his trip, we had a meeting and he brought up the incident with the commissioner. I disagreed with the Dutchman's philosophy on how to run a hotel. We mutually agreed to terminate our contract. One year was enough for me with the wild Dutchman.

Meanwhile, Gene McDaniel, the insurance adjuster for the worker's compensation case for the Riverfront, called and left a message. He requested a meeting—three weeks after the alleged accident. I met Gene at the hotel and we reviewed the case. He felt that the insurance company could get off with a small settlement. He continued by saying that his workload was extremely backlogged.

I said, "Wait a minute! Thomas and I have had a surveillance on Harry for two weeks. He was spotted carrying a fifty-pound bag of dog food out of the supermarket." I told Gene to drag out the case because Thomas and I would have evidence that this was a fraudulent claim. Gene agreed to work with us since we were doing his job. I was selfish because any claims the hotel filed would increase its premiums. Harry hired an ambulance chaser to file suit against the hotel. Of course, the way our justice system worked and the way our courts were backed up, we had plenty of time to prove our case.

The next time Thomas observed Harry, he was wearing a neck and back brace. We continued to observe Harry during different times of each day of the week. It took us a few weeks of photographing Harry being involved in different activities that would put pressure on the back muscles. On several occasions, Harry would come out of his house, thoroughly look around, and remove his neck collar. Thomas filmed Harry working on his car, repairing his roof gutters, and cutting his lawn. I followed Harry to his favorite country-and-western bar. Harry did enjoy his longneck beers with a shot of liquor. I took a quiet, out-of-the-way table in the corner of the bar to observe my employee. As the evening progressed, Harry began to get loose. The more he drank, the more he danced and the more pictures I snapped.

The next day I called Gene and presented him with the photos and the file that Thomas and I had compiled. He was very surprised and grateful. About a week later, Gene called and advised us that the insurance company had filed a counterclaim and were pursuing a charge of insurance fraud. I was shocked when Gene informed me that insurance fraud exceeded twenty billion dollars per year! What's wrong with America?

As mentioned previously, the booming Disney area attracted all walks of life. Jo-Jo called me from Kissimmee and advised me that another guest had been robbed. I called David, the manager, at the Quality Inn and told him that I was headed to the property. When I arrived, the police were finishing their report. I reviewed the incident with David and Sgt. Lewis, the officer in charge. He informed us that this was the fourth attack on tourists in the area, and that this was similar to the robberies in Miami. It was assumed that the criminals would park in the hotel's lot and stake out unsuspecting tourists. As the hotel guests got out of their vehicles, the assailants would walk up behind them and force them into their room. The thieves would slap the people to show force and then ransack their belongings. They would threaten the vacationers with their lives and would make their getaway.

The next morning, I called a staff meeting to inform the employees of the previous night's happening. I told David to hire a person for the evening shift to serve as security and maintenance. A couple weeks passed with two more robberies in the area. Then in the third week from our terrible ordeal, The *Sentinel*'s second-page headline was, "Tourist Thieves Nabbed." The article said that the lowlifes had come from California. The story continued by saying that similar crimes had occurred in that state. If the bleeding hearts would not interfere, then perhaps justice could be served as it should!

Speaking of hotel security and safety, for some reason a few hotel visitors acted like babies when they walked through the lobby doors. These particular few individuals wanted to sue the hotel if they stubbed their little toe. They would always have advice for the staff. Some states were making it mandatory to install sprinkler systems throughout older hotels. All hotels and motels had sensitive smoke detectors. It took 180 degrees to set off the sprinkler system, which is a little late. When a fire alarm or smoke detector would go off everything would stop to be investigated. As usual, the government forced hotel owners to install a very expensive, unnecessary system. If a fire did not ruin the hotel, the sprinkler system would complete the job! The new electronic locks with the computer cards revolutionized security in the hospitality industry. If the manager or the maintenance chief did change a lock when a key was lost, that was an excellent practice. If they didn't, that was very dangerous and the property could have been liable. Most of the keys would have the room number and a tag advertising the hotel. Hello? All hotels have or should have safety deposit boxes for valuables and be free to the guests.

I would like to mention a couple of experiences about safety. At the Quality Inn, a carpet seam was loose and torn (admittedly, it should have been repaired). A guest tripped and claimed an injury. Our liability insurance company settled out of court for twenty thousand dollars. At the Riverfront Hotel, we had a guest who was very inebriated and fell up the stairs. Yes, she fell up—she missed a step up and hit her chin, knee, and breasts. That was her story. Our room clerk witnessed her coming into the hotel and swore the guest could not stand up. She refused medical attention and checked out the next morning. Ten days later the hotel heard from her attorney. She made the statement that the lighting was bad or was out in the stairway. She forgot to mention that she was drunk as a Saturday night redneck. The case was dismissed.

At all my hotels, I stressed the importance of the safety and security of our guests. Most managers felt as I did—safety and security was everyone's responsibility.

The reason some guests left their responsibilities at home was because of the competitive hotel franchise companies. Granted, some hotels/motels should not have had their franchise signs—e.g., some older Holiday Inns. Within the corporate maze, the young, yuppie, nonoperating, experienced marketing "experts" began creating 100 percent guaranteed satisfaction! The corporate franchisees continued to spoil the demanding public. The old sayings, "If you give an inch, they'll take a mile," or

"The more you give, the more they want," are true. First it was soap and a towel—now it is two types of soaps, shampoo, conditioner, lotion, all sizes of towels (bath towels are fifty inches long), facial tissue, sewing kits, in-room coffee, movies, shoeshine kits, mints, fruit baskets, clock radios, whirlpool tubs, mouthwash, combs, toothbrushes with toothpaste, razors, shaving cream, deodorant, rollaways, cribs, drinking glasses, room service, microwaves, refrigerators, hair dryers, irons with ironing boards, two television sets, two telephones (one in bathroom) with data ports, fax machines, secretary services, baby-sitting services, airport shuttle, free breakfast, free cocktails, and even robes! Where is it going to stop? Why do the guests have so much luggage since the hotels provide so much?

Not only has the work force changed, hotel guests were changing. While at the Quality Inn, I overheard a conversation at the front desk. Mr. Pierce, a hotel guest, was bickering with Jill, the front-office manager. Since Jill was a professional, I did not interrupt the debate. I heard Mr. Pierce say, "I don't understand why you don't take my credit card." Jill in her smooth Southern manner reminded the guest that she was not refusing his card, the system would not approve the amount requested. Mr. Pierce continued to fuss with Jill as he said, "I sent my credit card payment over a week ago!" The man continued until Manny and I walked into the scene.

I asked, "Is there anything I can help you with, sir?"

With a snarl, he answered, "Show this broad how to clear my card!"

I snapped, "First, Miss O'Brien is not a broad, and second, we do not keep track of your credit, and third, the Holiday Inn is just down the street!"

The man left swearing at us as he stomped out of the lobby. What happened to the good old days when guests would check in the hotel and pay upon checking out? Why do some guests get angry with the hotel staff when credit cards are not approved? The systems decline the charge, not the room clerks!

Another interesting trend of the hotel business is the guest traveling with pets. Hotels and motels are guilty of encouraging this because of competition. While managing the Ramada (when Victor was on vacation), I experienced an unusual event. Gilberto from the front desk called me and said that he had a situation. I went to the front desk to investigate. Gilberto and Manny, the security guard, were discussing the situation. They relayed what was happening. Neighboring guests were complaining with noise from Room 118. Gilberto called the room with no answer. Manny said that the Do Not Disturb sign was on the door. I asked Manny to accompany me to the room. I knocked loudly and said, "Security." No answer. I repeated my actions. I opened the door, and we entered to view a destroyed room. About this time a large chimpanzee leaped upon Manny's back and a brightly colored parrot flew in front of my face. The animals were cute and playful as we tried to herd them toward their cages. After bribing the mischievous playmates back into their cages, the owners walked into the room. They were startled and began to get hostile toward Manny and myself. I identified myself, and the Latin duo calmed themselves. I continued by asking, "Will you clean the room and pay damages?"

They both nodded and said, "Yes, sir, and we are sorry for the mess."

Since the hotel allowed pets, we were at the mercy of the guests. Upon checking the room when the guests vacated, we had to replace the carpet, a chair and two lamps. The guests sneaked out of the hotel in the middle of the night. The housekeeper told us that they picked up the animals in Miami and were taking them to a circus. Of course, most pets are cats and dogs, but on occasions I had seen snakes, monkeys, rodents, ocelots, birds, frogs, fish, a small pony, and a llama! Where would it stop—no pets!

I decided that I must adjust to the changing computer age ever since Jo-Jo called me a dinosaur. I refused to be an Eighties-Nineties yuppie by driving a little BMW with an ever-so-important cellular phone in my ear. I did carry a pager because of my responsibilities.

A few quiet months passed without any major incidents. I observed another interesting trait of the traveling public. While visiting the Riverfront Hotel, I saw Thomas take a call from a former guest. She was complaining that she left a gown and that the hotel had not returned the garment. Thomas explained that the hotel maintained a lost-and-found log and that he did not find the item listed. He assured the lady, who had checked out two days previously, that he would personally investigate the matter. The very sincere Thomas searched the housekeeping department and located a pink gown. Thomas called the lady to tell her the news and informed her that would send it C.O.D. Well, that would not do! The woman became rather arrogant with Thomas as if it was his fault she left the gown. She continued by acting insulted because the hotel did not pay the postage! I took the telephone and explained that we were here to rent good clean rooms with Southern hospitality, but that we were not parents of our guests.

Each time that I approached the Ramada, I had an uneasy feeling. I arrived late, walked around the property, and checked in. The next morning I met Victor for breakfast. Later we reviewed the latest financial statement. The property had turned around to be a very profitable operation.

Victor received a call from the housekeeping department. Maria, the executive housekeeper, was very excited and said that we needed to come to her office ASAP! Victor and I ran over to housekeeping, and when we entered we were in for a shocking surprise. Hector Hernadez, a houseman, had all the housekeepers, laundry workers, and Maria sitting together on the floor. Hector was a quiet, middle-aged Cuban who worked hard but did act strange at times. He was waving a .38 pistol and in a very tense, broken English voice said, "You can't fire me!"

Victor responded in a calm Spanish voice by saying, "Hector, what are you talking about?"

Hector said, "Juan told me that I was going to get fired!" Juan worked in maintenance and was Hector's cousin. They argued constantly.

Victor and I assured Hector that we weren't firing him and that he needed to put the gun down. I asked Hector not to turn this into a major hostage situation. Victor continued to reason with him and reminded him of his family. I made a move to the coffee pot and Hector pointed the gun directly toward my face. I smiled and said, "Hector, I am just getting a cup of coffee. Can I get you one?" He nodded yes.

I poured two cups of coffee and slowly headed toward Hector. Victor continued to talk to the disturbed man while moving closer to him. Hector's voice began to crack in a calm manner as tears began to trickle down his rough face. I took one of his hands and put the cup of coffee in it while Victor took the gun out of the other hand. We all sat down as I told the other employees to hurry out. Victor and I continued to comfort Hector while he cried and talked nonsense.

The front desk had called the local police. As we walked out, the SWAT team rushed up to us and began to manhandle Hector. I said, "Wait a minute! Don't mistreat this man. He needs help!"

After the investigation, some interesting facts came to light. Hector had come from Cuba just two years before going to work at the hotel. The records showed that he came over during the big exodus on anything that floated. That was the time that Castro emptied some prisons and institutions. After all was said and done, I was truly thankful that no one got hurt. Since employees of post offices, stockbrokers' offices, and other businesses have gone berserk and shot up their places of work, we were lucky!

I called Jo-Jo and said that I would be home soon. When I arrived at my beach office home, I took a long weekend and reviewed our life and situation. Jo-Jo and I decided to sell our lake home in Kissimmee. She was in complete agreement that I needed a long vacation. Jo-Jo began to plan our English and European holiday while I concluded our business.

As I drove between properties I began wondering if all businesses had the inspectors that hotels had to entertain. We had inspectors from local, state, and federal agencies. We had elevator, pool, fire, health, and beverage inspectors. We had rating (e.g., AAA), franchisee, and owner inspections. Above all the guest was the most important!

My mind would continue to go back to our double-standard government. Government officials are forbidden from accepting gifts or incentives. This does not hold true with hotels. All hotel chains offer some type of a frequent stay program. The traveling government employee accumulates the points for free stays as our government pays the bills! The employee uses the free nights for personal vacations. Shame on us!

The hospitality business had definitely changed, as did our way of life. The traveling public was getting confused with all the new franchise brands in the marketplace. The traveling public had become extremely demanding while the labor force had deteriorated. The computer had changed our way of life. What would the balance of the Nineties bring in our new technology era?

CHAPTER 9

SOUTH FLORIDA

1995

"Mr. Wayne, I need you down here now!" said a very excited Victor.

I asked, "What was the problem?" Even though Victor was a fiery, emotional Latin, he was a very capable and logical innkeeper. He continued by saying that Mr. Vega, one of the owners, had been in the Ramada for two days. Victor related that Mr. Vega had become a nuisance by excess drinking in the lounge, complaining to the employees, and making sexual advances toward guests and employees. I told Victor that I was on my way!

While driving to the property I began to formulate a plan on how to handle Mr. Vega. This situation was difficult to understand since Mr. Vega was always the quiet, older gentleman of the investor's group. I arrived early evening and immediately began looking for Victor. I located Victor and we headed to Salsa, our cocktail lounge. There we spotted Mr. Vega at the end of the bar. As Victor and I approached him with a big smile, I said, "Mr. Vega, it is so good to see you again."

Mr. Vega replied, "Chance, good to see you. Let's have a drink."

The lounge was having a packed cocktail hour. I said, "Okay, but let's go somewhere else. I do not like to drink on property." He looked puzzled but agreed. On the way out of the lobby I tried to convince Mr. Vega to have some coffee and something to eat. He became belligerent and said, "Don't try to trick me like everyone else!"

I immediately said, "No, sir. Let's walk over to Bennigan's." I told Victor that he could go home because we would be fine.

As Mr. Vega and I had a cocktail, he began to tell me his problems. He opened up by saying that his wife and his girlfriend were having affairs. A sad, drunken, middle-aged man continued to ramble about his difficulties. Mr. Vega enlightened me to the fact that the investment group was having financial trouble. Not only did they own the hotel, their portfolio included apartment buildings, warehouses, shopping centers, fishing fleets, and a cannery. I began talking to Mr. Vega as a friend. After a couple of hours, his attitude became positive, and he agreed to vacate the hotel.

The next morning I met Victor and Mr. Vega for breakfast. We continued our conversation about the hotel. I asked if it was for sale. He said that will probably happen in the new few months. I asked Mr. Vega to give me first option. He agreed and left the inn. Victor thanked me and we headed toward his office. I made a package of the property to present to Mr. John Sheffield.

After receiving the package, John called me and said that he would be interested in purchasing the Ramada. I then contacted Mr. Vega to inform him of a possible purchaser. Phone tag went on between the two parties for several weeks. I did not get an agreement for a real estate contract—again trusting everyone.

Meanwhile back at the Riverside in Melbourne, Thomas told me that the eccentric author Ted Anderson had moved in to the hotel. Over a short period of time, Ted and I became drinking friends. At times he appeared to be insane but he was fun to be around. Ted was so overbearing at times, Thomas could not handle him. I would have to counsel Ted as a friend and a son. Once Ted called a taxi to drive him to McDonald's (two blocks) and drop him back at the hotel's swimming pool. He gave the driver a fifty-dollar tip to wait for one hour.

Ted was a tall, handsome, blonde, educated man in his thirties. All my female employees favored him while the male employees disliked him. Of course he dated the employees. The other problem I had with Ted was that he would light up a joint in the lounge. The last straw was when Ted came to the front desk naked and dripping wet. He screamed at the front-desk clerk that he had not received any housekeeping service for several days. Tracey apologized and said that the "Do Not Disturb" sign has been on the door for days. She then threw two pool towels toward Ted.

The next morning I went by the hotel to ask Ted to leave. While Thomas and I were having breakfast in the coffee shop, we spotted Ted helping a senior couple with their luggage. Thomas and I stared at one another with stunned expressions. After Ted wished the couple a nice day, he joined us. I began to explain how we operate the hotel professionally. Before I could ask him to leave, Ted pleaded with us not to throw him out. Thomas and I agreed to just one more tantrum!

While visiting the Quality Inn, Jill, the MOD, called me about 2:00 A.M. to inform me of a situation. I scampered to get dressed and run downstairs. When I arrived at the desk, Jill met and advised me why the paramedics were on property. Spring break increased occupancy as well as situations. The hotel had a college student group check in for a couple of days. After sleeping in hotels for years, noise never bothered me. The group had been partying and had taken their activity down by the pool. A dare had been issued and a young man (who was high on something) jumped from a third-floor balcony trying to reach the swimming pool. While the paramedics rushed the young man out, some of his "friends" were still laughing and partying. I told the policemen to disperse the people ASAP or arrest them. They did, and I asked them to call us about the condition of the crazy boy. The next day I received a call from the parents of the silly young man. They informed me that he was in serious condition with two broken legs, broken ribs, and some internal bleeding. They thanked us for our response and concern.

I had an upcoming meeting with the owner in two days and I felt that I had worked myself out of a contract again. This came true but the Inn was not sold, the owner's family was going to manage the property. The changeover went smoothly and efficiently. One down and two to go!

Back to Florida's east coast to see one of Jo-Jo's shows. Jo-Jo founded a group of tap dancers known as the Gold Diggers. They were performing benefit shows up and down the coast. She was back to her love—the theatre.

Dealing with the traveling public and the work force, I felt that I had to be a man of many faces.

Early Monday morning, I headed south on the ever congested I-95. For the first time, I did not have an uneasy feeling as I approached the Ramada Inn. Victor and I had an early, quiet dinner. I had a good, solid night's sleep. The next afternoon was quite different and exciting. We had a Brazilian tour group, a church group, business people, seniors, and other vacationers registered in the hotel. Victor had to leave the property for a meeting. Ricardo from the front desk called me about a situation at the pool. As I headed directly toward the pool area, I noticed a crowd at the front desk. When I arrived at poolside, I had an inside chuckle. Upon the scene, I saw about fifteen women with no bathing suit tops and several well-tanned pudgy men wearing thongs. They were swimming, diving, and sun bathing. The church group was having a fit. I stood back and enjoyed the scenery before I called the tour director. The director got her clients back in their tops. The church people settled down and were crowded together at one end of the pool while the Brazilians continued to frolic.

The next day I met with Mr. Vega, and he informed me that the investors group had accepted a contract. The deal closed in thirty days, and the Sheffield group took over immediately. I received a finder's fee, not a commission, and again was out of a job.

Mr. Patel, the owner of the Riverside Hotel, had left a message for me to reach him ASAP. I met him at the hotel and he advised me that he was giving up the property to the lienholder. He said that he recommended them to retain my services to manage the hotel. Since I knew that

Patel was a scamp, I had no faith in that happening. Within four months I lost three management contracts. Each hotel takes a small piece of your soul.

CHAPTER 10

WEST PALM BEACH

1997

After a well-deserved vacation, I called my friend Bryan Anderson. He was a regional director with Remington Hotels, a hotel management company out of Dallas. They were concentrating on the development of Embassy Suites. Within two weeks, Bryan phoned and offered me the innkeeper's position at the West Palm Beach Embassy Suites. The property was absolutely beautiful with its atrium featuring open-air dining and bar, ponds with bridges over waterfalls, and two elegant swans—Bach and Beethoven. The suites were well appointed with all the amenities. The hotel was located in an excellent area at the intersection of I-95 and PGA Boulevard. The staff was adequate considering the status of the labor market. It was a pleasure to work with Bryan, but a couple of department heads proved to be untrustworthy and disloyal. Within a few weeks, tension began to mount between the front desk and the sales department. Normally in most hotels the sales departments fight with the food and beverage departments.

It did not take long before I realized that the sales office had a hot line to the corporate office in Dallas. With the uneasy atmosphere I felt as if I was in a spy movie. Sandra, the sales manager, made life very difficult for Bill, the front-office manager. Bill was a fine, dedicated young man in his late twenties. He was an asset to me because he taught me the property management and reservation systems. Again I was in a peacemaker's position rather than a manager's position. It appeared that Sandra was forcing Bill to quit or get fired.

Even though every time I walked into the hotel I felt stressed, Jo-Jo and I enjoyed our life and new home. We lived and played at the PGA development. Jo-Jo and I cherished the time we watched Hale Irwin win the Seniors PGA. Later that day we socialized with the professional golfers and media. My position did provide us with enjoyable perks. Jo-Jo continued her dancing and performed in shows with the Ziegfeld Girls.

I had Thomas working with me again and we lived close to our best friends Gail and Bill. Good friends visited us on a regular basis, especially the golfers. The only thing wrong—I was very unhappy at my work. I had a neat boss but a treacherous company. The very young corporate leaders had no idea what the word "hospitality" meant or about the art of innkeeping.

In previous years I had experienced micromanagement, but this company had raised it to a new height. The corporate "experts" required the staff to have daily yield management meetings. Get this—we had to call and include them in a conference call. This was the first hotel that we would change rates by the hour! Our rates could vary from $69 to $299. Dallas even began planning our rates for the 1999 Super Bowl to be held in Miami. I heard $500 per night, even though we were in North Palm

Beach, not Miami! This is known as gouging. I could see the reasons that Bill had trouble keeping a staff at the front desk. The front-office clerks did not know what to quote as a rate at any given time. Hell, we were all confused. Each day there were consultations with unhappy guests. It is easy for the boys in the corporate office to say, "Handle it." No one liked to go to work and have the customers in their face as a daily routine. For this reason I had tried to avoid working for large, greedy corporations.

I reluctantly began to contemplate seeking other employment. I needed a change for mental health purposes. The company paid well but not enough for the stress. Even though we had the good life, time came to be a real innkeeper again.

I previously mentioned the demanding public, well—in Palm Beach we had more than our share. One guest and her family absolutely became a nuisance to the staff. Mrs. Abernathy wanted to be in the suite with the housekeeper to ensure that it was cleaned to her standard. She demanded evening turndown service with extra mints. She called my office to find out why she and her family could not have breakfast room service—free! Embassy Suites offered a lovely complimentary buffet breakfast to their guests. We had a room service menu available. Mrs. A. continued to give Bill a hard time. In our hotel brochure it stated that baby-sitting was available. She interpreted it to mean the hotel provided this service. She refused to call the childcare service and instructed Bill to do so. To top it off, she expected the hotel to pay the fee!

At check-out Mrs. A. insisted on several discounts, complained about the costs of telephone calls, and said she did not receive her wake-up calls. Bill stood strong about no free room. She then demanded to see me. I went to the front desk to see this pain in the ass. I first explained that any discounts offered must be requested at check-in. Then I told the lady all hotels mark up telephone calls and that her bill was correct. I apologized to her that she did not hear the wake-up call. Mrs. A. saw that she could not con me so she became louder. As usual, she wanted the name of my boss and the address of the corporate office. As I gave the woman the information I said, "Mrs. Abernathy, don't forget my name, Chance Wayne, and don't misspell it. Please leave the hotel and have a nice day, so we may have one!" The other guests and staff applauded as I walked away.

A few weeks later, Bryan told me that he was resigning and he thought the property was being sold. That evening I began faxing my resumé to a few selected companies.

On one weekend we had a couple of little boys' soccer teams in the hotel. They ran security and me ragged. I do not know why parents let their children run wild in hotels. The boys were running up and down the halls to and from the swimming pool. John the security guard and I did have a little revenge.

The cheeky little ringleader had been running around the lobby as well as up and down the spiral staircase. In a few minutes, we heard little Johnny screaming. John and I glanced up to the second floor that overlooked the lobby and spotted little Johnny. He had caught his head in the railing. As he screamed, John smiled at me and we casually headed upstairs. When we arrived to free the brat, we spotted three or four water balloons. I said, "Young man, stop screaming and squirming and we will free you."

John had a great sense of humor (he had several grandchildren). He winked at me and said, "Mr. Wayne, I think we need to shave his head and trim his ears." Little Johnny started screaming louder. We pried the rails and released the little boy. We tried to talk to him but he ran toward his room. I called his parents and they grew very defensive with me. Of course, we had complaints from other hotel guests. Parents, keep your children under control while in a hotel. Hotels are also a place of rest, not a playground or a running track.

For centuries, innkeepers have invited their guests to make themselves at home. In our modern times, our guests have taken this practice to the extreme. On a Tuesday morning, I met a representative from the LPGA for breakfast. As we were discussing the future tournament, we both stopped talking and stared at incoming restaurant guests. We smiled at one another and ordered our coffee. The shocking sight of the vacationing family damned near knocked us off breakfast. Gary, the golf representative, laughed and said, "Hell if I wanted to see that—I could have stayed home." The mother and daughter had those sausage-looking curlers in their hair. They were wearing robes and fuzzy slippers. The father looked as if he had just stepped out of bed. His hair was sticking straight up, no shave and wearing pajamas with no shoes. The two little boys were in swimsuits with no shoes. This was a very nice restaurant serving a delicious buffet in an elegant atmosphere. It was extremely busy with our corporate clientele. I had learned not to be surprised at anything I heard or saw in a hotel. We continued to laugh and finished our meal and our deal.

Within a couple of weeks, I had a call from Dallas. The young yuppie vice president asked me if I was looking for another job. I told him that with the uneasy atmosphere I needed to leave. Before he could arrive, I discovered that someone in the sales department informed the corporate office that I was faxing my resumé to other companies. The interoffice and corporate politics was ridiculous to the point of being humorous.

I had been looking for a small company or a small property in order that I could be a happy, sane innkeeper. Before I left the Embassy Suites, I had offers as a hotel director of operations, a partnership in a cocktail lounge and restaurant, and an innkeeper's position. The innkeeper's job was in the Midwest. A small company from Illinois was building small hotels in Illinois and Indiana. This appealed to me because the properties were new and the ownership was solid. The president of the company was a knowledgeable hotel person. He checked me out as I checked the company out. This looked like a good match. Mr. Dowell drove to Palm Beach and interviewed me at the Embassy Suites during my last week of employment. Within one week, Mr. Dowell offered me an attractive package. Jo-Jo reluctantly agreed and we accepted. Next stop would be the land of Lincoln.

CHAPTER 11

SPRINGFIELD, IL

1998

Illinois was not the same or even vaguely close to the West Palm Beach scene but as everyone says, "Midwest people are so nice." This was true for most of the people that Jo-Jo and I met. Even though I had operated hotels in Indiana and Illinois in the past, this was still another culture shock for us. We knew to expect a cold winter, a welcomed spring, a steamy summer and a colorful fall.

As we traveled north from Marion to Springfield, Jo-Jo and I felt as if the corn fields were closing in on us. The bright spot was our return visit to St. Louis. On a glorious sunny day we frolicked under the Arch, toured the city and romanced by the Mississippi River. While visiting the River Queen Casino Boat, I learned of even more ridiculous state gambling laws. We had to buy a boarding ticket and wait until the next sailing—that never left the dock! After I won a few hundred dollars at Blackjack and Jo hitting a $100 jackpot on the slots, we went to the Solard area for a nightcap. Late that night we arrived at the Comfort Suites in Springfield.

The next morning I began my usual review of the staff and inspection of the property. The Comfort Suites was a quaint three-year old, three-story hotel conveniently located for the traveler. The General Manager was not there but the young Assistant Manager showed me the property. Roberta was a dedicated young lady that had been with the company since her school days. She was sweet but I felt resentment from her. This was due to two reasons—she thought she should have been promoted to General Manager and she had to vacate the Manager's apartment. Of course, through my career, I have experienced this situation several times. Mr. Dowell asked me to put professionalism throughout the hotel beginning with Roberta.

After a week, I felt that I knew the type of staff that I had inherited—an unhappy, disrespectful Executive Housekeeper that could not keep a dependable staff, a Chief Engineer that was good when he was at work, a sweet, talkative Breakfast Hostess, and undependable Front Desk staff. The Front Desk staff was a strange crew. One lazy young man (Dick) was receiving child support from his ex-wife, receiving financial help from the State and always complaining. Another young man (Leon) was ambitious but always breaking company policy. Leon was loved by the guests—particularly the girls. He was our local Casanova. The young college ladies were good and somewhat dependable. Art, the Night Auditor, was stereotypically, moody. There was absolutely no sales and marketing efforts in effect. To be such a nice little property, it needed a good cleaning. Even though this was the smallest property that I had ever operated, I would still write a business and marketing plan.

Even though Springfield is a Midwest conservative city and the state's capital, I did meet some interesting characters. I implemented my business and marketing plan and tried to inspire the Housekeeper. The Front Desk was capable enough but again, attitude had to change. They were unprofessional and very nonchalant. An example of this was when Leon, while on duty as the Relief Night Auditor, went "skinny dipping" during the middle of the night. The local delivery newspaper woman was rather attractive and built well. I felt that they had a "thing going on." As long as it didn't effect his work, I didn't mind. When a guest mentions incidents, this is when it is serious! Leon was a clever lad because he even shut off the pool camera. So I had no hard evidence. When Leon came to work again, he naturally denied the incident. I knew he did it and I knew I had to watch him. What was bad, was the fact that I liked Leon and I knew he could be a good hotel man. It would be only a matter of time before "he hung himself."

As the months passed so did the employees. We had a 300% turnover in personnel. I continued to stay active in the community and make sales calls. Jo-Jo had become involved with the local theater and dance communities. She has always been an asset in helping me build business. Sales slowly continued to increase but establishing a good stable staff was a constant battle. I would never have dreamed a town like Springfield would have such a low unemployment rate. It appeared as if everyone worked or was waiting to go to work for the State. It was impossible to compete with the State. The State paid higher wages and offered outrageous benefits for a half of a day's work. Illinois is no different from other governmental domains. They create no revenue, continue to raise expenses, do favors for friends and relatives, continue to get larger, be ineffective and have forgotten they work for the people!

Speaking of characters, we had several State Representatives staying with us. The Chicago contingency was a group of "beauties." They acted as if they owned the hotel. They had to have special rooms, complimentary rides to the Capital building and they treated the Front Desk staff as their personal staff. As I got to know them, I found more and more what I should not have known. Representative Harold Miller would have late night female visitors, always a bottle of rum on hand and went to the Capital when he felt like showing up. Harold let me know that he owned a motel in another state. With his state having a personal income tax, I asked where the tax went. He didn't know. State income tax is another form of double taxation. That was the only state that I had paid an income tax! When will double standards cease?

Choice Hotels International has a frequent traveler's program known as Guest Privileges. The program was designed for legitimate travelers paying standard rack rates. The state employees demanded and paid the lowest rates. In turn the state employees accumulated the points and received the complimentary stays for their own personal use. Another Representative from Chicago told me, "Chance, it's a job—somebody has to do it. Where can you give yourselves raises with great benefits and work when you want?" Oh well, it's the American way.

Our little hotel began to set a precedent. Monday through Thursday we were filled with corporate people and State employees. We loved the corporate traveler. They were in one to three nights, minimum use of the room, left a tip, checked out (seldom a complaint) and made a future reservation. The weekend travelers were something else. We had them from all walks of life. The families, the seniors, AAA members, sport teams, church groups, wedding parties, family reunions, meetings, birthday parties, highway travelers, local rendezvous and the tourists that made my staff laugh and cry each weekend. Periodically we would have someone that never stayed in a hotel. They were cute and showed their appreciation. Gene and Jacquie Hayes became our best friends and introduced us around the business community. We broke the monotony by taking road trips to Chicago, St. Louis, Hannibal, Branson and Arthur, IL. Arthur is a quaint little Amish town that once a year has the "Pumpkin Patch" (and the best apple butter, butter and breads). On one of our visits to Branson, I experienced a forbidden policy in the hotel industry. Being hospitality people we knew not to try to check in early. We arrived after 4:00 p.m., waited and finally registered. The Front Desk staff appeared quite confused which we did understand. Jo-Jo and I were talking as we opened the door and to our surprise we heard sounds. They were pleasurable moans of enjoyment. We immediately backed out of the room. The couple did not notice. We went back to the Front Desk to advise them that the room was occupied. We were assigned another room. You won't believe that as we opened the door, we heard a deep male voice say, "Honey, is that you?" I responded in a high Spanish accented voice, "Sorry sir, housekeeping." Jo-Jo and I began laughing and ran back to the lobby. We sent a staff member to find an unoccupied room. I found out that they had lost their computer with no back up system or plan. A no, no...

After I visited other hotels, I always learned and appreciated something new. When I returned to my hotel I reviewed the business and reservations. Most franchise companies require a complimentary breakfast. This is a good time for a manager to meet his guests. This is similar to the old bed and breakfast inns but on a larger scale. At times this can be an entertaining experience. I have seen some interesting sights—ladies with large rollers (which looked like sausages) in their head, adults wearing animal fluffy slippers, grown men in pajamas and wearing no shoes (of course, not shaven and having bad breath), children in only bathing suits, extroverted women parading in see thru negligee. One Saturday morning while feeding the masses, everyone stopped and stared. I was at the Front Desk speaking with a guest. He excused himself and stared toward the breakfast room. A middle aged, well stacked woman came from the pool area and strutted across the room. The attractive lady was wearing high heeled shoes and a thong bathing suit!

As I mentioned before, the traveling public has gotten very demanding. Even with a complimentary deluxe continental breakfast (without meat and eggs) the guests asked for more and more. An example was milk. Guests requested skim milk, 1% milk, 2% milk, whole milk, buttermilk, chocolate mix and even goat's milk! Cereals! Has anyone counted the cereals and pastries that are in the supermarket? Come on, it was free!

Speaking of swimming pools, every guest wants to know that the hotel has one. It appears that only ten percent of the guests even use the pool or fitness room. We did have a guest that was a dedicated fitness "nut." David was a handsome, young black man from Chicago. He worked out in the fitness room and then swam a few laps in the pool. Lillie and Vosha (housekeeping) pointed him out to Valerie at the Front Desk. She in turn told me about him. David had come straight out of the pool and began a vigorous walk through the halls of the hotel. What was unusual about this was the fact that he had a large erection in front of his wet shorts. No problem, he kept on walking, smiled and spoke to the ladies. Of course, David became known as "The Viagra Kid".

There's always something going on in a hotel. One quiet Thursday afternoon the fire alarm system went off. The system showed it was on the third floor. I raced up the stairs to that area. As I approached the third floor I smelled something cooking and noticed smoke coming from under our apartment door. Jo-Jo was preparing blackened salmon. She had no idea that she caused the commotion. I went back to the office and silenced the alarm. I called the fire station and advised that it was a false alarm. The firemen arrived shortly and checked the panel. I told them that some lady (I did not mention that it was my wife) had set it off due to cooking. They knocked on our door and scared Jo-Jo to death. They reset the system and left. I had a good laugh and a great meal!

Reservations has taken a new turn—the Internet. Being an old Innkeeper, I tried to adjust. Reservations were made when a guest left (repeat business) the hotel, through a travel agent, by telephone, fax or letter. Since the Internet has become a way of life, the cyber junkies think they are getting a deal. Mr. John Sutton made a reservation through the Net and received a 5% discount. The same day he called four times to ask questions. The toll free numbers are not the answer because the reservationists will say anything to book a room. Travel agents are just that –agents. Remember, requests are just that—to ask for. The best way to make a reservation is to call the hotel direct and ask for all requests—smoking or non-smoking, king or doubles, poolside, higher floor, ground floor, handicap, pets, free breakfast, directions, shopping, restaurants, pool, amenities, etc. I recommend to always get a confirmation number and a name.

There are strength in numbers. This is the philosophy of groups in hotels. In the spring of '99, we had cheerleading groups in from Chicago for the State competition. The largest group took 25 rooms and decided to take over the hotel (which they did). We had a rooming list but it didn't matter because they switched rooms with each other. The teenagers ran up and down the hallways and had meetings in the stairways all night. I called the parents but they were drinking and partying as well. Before I got downstairs the next morning (8:00 a.m.) the mothers were reliving their youth. They had moved all the lobby furniture into a corner. The frustrated mothers were dressed in "cute little" uniforms and struggling through cheers. One lady was on the second floor directing the show. This was another new experience. The lobby was adjacent to the breakfast room and close to the first floor rooms. What was an Innkeeper to do? While they were having a good time, the other hotel guests were complaining. I spoke to the leader and she had the audacity to get upset.

In the spring of 2000, we had a group of female bowlers. They were a fun bunch too. I had a guest call my office to tell me that a loud group of women were putting golf balls the length of the hallway. I went to investigate and sure enough, a putting competition was in progress. I told them to quiet down and break up the game. They booed me and offered me a drink and more. I tried to be firm but they were comical. They finished the final bet and broke up. I have always wondered, why some adults do not know how to act when they get away from home.

Of course, this hotel could not escape without its own disasters. One very cold winter, we lost power. Naturally it was in the evening—no lights or heat. As the night progressed the guests began to get restless. We used every blanket and bed pad in the hotel. The lobby was full by the fireplace. I always keep flashlights on hand. Most guests were understanding but a few were even more demanding. In a couple of hours the electricity came on and all went back to normal. The next morning, the not so reasonable people brought down the 100% guarantee cards. Of course they demanded free rooms. I said, "Absolutely not, it was an act of nature, can't you see the three feet of snow outside?" They took my business cards in order that they could file a complaint.

One weekend, the Front Desk began to receive phone calls from the guests—no hot water! This was serious—no hot shower or shave! Sure enough, I checked the hot water gauges—60 degrees and dropping. I immediately called the plumber. He arrived within a couple of hours. Being a Saturday morning, he could not get the mixing valve that was needed. He rigged the system to get me by until the next week. This incident cost the hotel about ten free stays. We got off lucky. This type of incident always happens on weekends or at night.

One Sunday morning I went down to the Front Desk to help out. It was extremely busy with guests checking out, the phones ringing and swimmers wanting towels. A strange looking lady was at the end of the counter, tipping her fingers and staring. Valerie asked to help her and she said that she needed to speak with the manager. In a couple of moments, I said, "Yes ma'am, may I help you?" She said, "Why do you have the housekeepers do the under roll?" I said, "What? I don't make my housekeepers exercise." With a serious stare, she said, "Sir, your toilet tissue comes from underneath and not over the top." I was stunned for a moment and thought she was joking. She was dead serious. I thought quick and said, "You are right but your housekeeper is left-handed. I feel the same way and I will correct the situation." She asked for a discount for the inconvenience. I refused and she went away mumbling to herself. When she was out of sight, I could not hold back the laughter. That was about the ultimate in guest comments.

Certain trade shows are important in the promoting of hotels. The local show known as "Business Connections" is a typical show. At all trade shows the exhibitors should be friendly and out going. Most complain while they are having a good time. It is fun to watch the guests. You have the ones that are talkative, the shy ones, the greedy ones (takes more than one sample), the ones that just stare, the sneaky ones and the little ladies that get a bag and go shopping. Sales is the name of game.

Springfield was good to Jo-Jo and I. The ownership of the hotel was appreciative and a pleasure to work with. For a monochromatic city that has a dead president as a tourist attraction the commerce is extremely good. With other activities such as the State Fair, the high school rodeo competition, livestock shows, State and Regional competitions, the Air Show and conventions, the city runs a high hotel occupancy. Even with its terrible weather, pot holes, corn fed kings and queens, smoke stacks and crooked politicians—the people are nice. A special thanks to my special staff.

The nineties had brought us overworked terms—politically correct, sexual harassment, Viagra, the internet, E-mail, voice mail, cellular phones, web sites, signing bonuses, free agents, CDs and Y2K! While the President faced impeachment about lying concerning his sexual misconduct, the Cold War died a natural death when the USSR became Russia again. NASA sent probes to Mars while the United States engaged in another undeclared war—the Persian Gulf War. While the theaters were reproducing major hits such as *The King and I*, Hollywood gave us such hits as *Silence of the Lambs* and *Dances With Wolves*. Television provided us with comedy laughs from *The Golden Girls* and *Cheers*.

Revolutionary changes had been taking place in the hospitality industry as well. Las Vegas became the city with the largest number of hotel rooms in the world. As Vegas continued to build, the MGM Grand Hotel became the largest hotel on the globe with over 5,000 rooms and suites! New York City continued to be the city with the highest room rate average. Because of space the Japanese had built stacked accommodations near major airports. The Four Seasons Hotels leads the list of only 17 five star hotels in the United States. Manufactured motels could be completed in twelve weeks. All major hotel/motel chains had resorted to franchising rather than investing their own capital. While the franchise companies continued to confuse the demanding traveling public, the labor force of the country became critical. What shall the new century bring to the hotel business? In 1969, Hilton promised to be the first hotel in space. I volunteered then to be the first Innkeeper in space . . . . .

In closing . . .

One day in heaven the Lord decided he would visit the earth, and take a stroll. Walking down the road, the Lord encountered a man who was crying. The Lord asked the man, "Why are you crying my son?" The man said he was blind and had never seen a sunset. The Lord touched the man and he could see and he was happy.

As the Lord walked further he met another crying man and asked, "Why are you crying my son?" The man was born a cripple and never able to walk. The Lord touched him and he could walk and he was happy.

Farther down the road the Lord met another man crying and asked, "Why are you crying my son?" The man said, "Lord I work for a hotel," and the Lord sat down and cried with him.

GENERAL GLOSSARY OF HOTEL TERMS

Advance Deposit: Payments received for future reservations

Bed Tax: Local resort (city or county) tax

Booked: The hotel is full for certain dates.

City Ledger: Accounts receivable

Comp: A complimentary room.

Curb Appeal: Neat and tidy outside grounds/landscaping to attract guests

Express Check-In: A speedy registration.

Express Check-Out: The night auditor checks out guest and guest does not go by front desk.

Flag: The franchise of a property.

The Folio: The balance sheet of charges and payments. Also a receipt.

Gouging: Taking advantage of the traveling public by over-charging (raising room rates).

A Guarantee: A room is guaranteed for late arrival—generally with a credit card.

Guarantee No-Show: A reservation (guest) that does not come in—hotel bills account.

Guest Ledger: In-house accounts receivable

In-house: Registered guests in hotel

MOD: Manager on Duty

No Show: A reservation (guest) that does not show.

Overbooking: To sell more rooms than a hotel has to accommodate.

Rack Rate: Standard published room rate

Skip: A guest who leaves a hotel owing a bill.

Walk: A guest who had a reservation but was sent to another hotel because of overbooking.

Walk-in: A guest without a reservation.

Yield Management: Maximizing room revenue

VIP: Very Important Person